Cecil Lewis was born in Birkenhead in 1898, joined the RFC in 1916 as a pilot and was awarded the MC. After the war he went to Peking to teach the Chinese to fly. All this is recorded in *Sagittarius Rising*, recognized as a First World War classic. Returning to London he became one of the five founding members of the BBC and Chairman of the Programme Board from 1922 to 1926. He went on to write books and radio plays, directed the first two films made of Bernard Shaw's plays, was called to Hollywood where he got an Oscar for his script of *Pygmalion*, went on to beachcomb in Tahiti and returned to flying duties in the RAF in the Second World War. In 1947 he flew his own aeroplane to S. Africa where he farmed sheep. Returning to New York to work for the United Nations in 1951, he was subsequently invited to join the staff of Associated Rediffusion when commercial television was set up in London a year later. He retired to Corfu in 1968. Among his other books are *Farewell to Wings, Never Look Back, Turn Right for Corfu* and *Gemini to Joburg*. At 91 he is still writing.

D1345015

Also by Cecil Lewis

Non-fiction

BROADCASTING FROM WITHIN
SAGITTARIUS RISING
THE TRUMPET IS MINE
FAREWELL TO WINGS
TURN RIGHT FOR CORFU
NEVER LOOK BACK
A WAY TO BE
GEMINI TO JOBURG

Fiction

CHALLENGE TO THE NIGHT
YESTERDAY'S EVENING
PATHFINDERS
THE GOSPEL ACCORDING TO JUDAS

THE DARK SANDS OF SHAMBALA

Cecil Lewis

SPHERE BOOKS LIMITED

A SPHERE BOOK

First published in Great Britain by Sphere Books Ltd 1989

ISBN 0 7474 0358 9

Printed and bound in Great Britain by
Cox & Wyman Ltd, Reading

Sphere Books Ltd
A Division of
Macdonald & Co. (Publishers) Ltd.
66/73 Shoe Lane, London EC4P 4AB

A member of Maxwell Pergamon Publishing Corporation plc

'It was like a child's cry in a thunderstorm
For the dream that was long in coming,
For the hopes so often deferred,
For the rest our labours deserved,
For the heaven our hearts longed for,
For perfection in this life . . .'

CHAPTER ONE

The Cessna swept round the shoulder of the mountain, losing height rapidly. The island was bigger than I'd thought. Then there was a bay with a wonderful curve of blue sea and the scimitar of sand. Peter dived down, levelled off over the water, swung right to line up with the shore and put her down smoothly. The aircraft rolled to a standstill.

We sat for a moment gazing at sand, sea and sky, the marvellous emptiness of it all.

'Well, here we are! Like the look of it?'

'Fabulous!'

'Mm . . . Not bad.'

'So strange, the dark sand!'

'Yes. Grows on you. Makes the place really unique. You'll see . . . Well, I must get back. I'll pick you up on Monday. Got your kit?' The engines were still running. I opened the door, pulled out my bag and stepped down onto the sand. It was blazing hot.

'I'll be here either early morning or late afternoon. Too bumpy midday!' he shouted. 'Don't worry if I'm a day late. Enjoy yourself!'

'I shall!' I snapped the door to and stepped back. Peter opened up and I turned my back to the blast of hot sand. By the time it had subsided, he was airborne. He swung out over the sea, doubled back and came shooting by over the water waving to me as he passed. Then he went up in a steep climb, shrank to a dot and disappeared.

I stood there listening to the sound of the engines till

they faded and the silence came back. There was no sound but the lapping of the water. I was alone. Quite alone. Alone on a desert island! Nobody but me on that great sweep of shore, the leaning palms, the lagoon, the surf boiling over the reef, the infinite horizon of sky and sea . . . and less than a week ago I was in London. I couldn't believe it. I just stood there, staring.

Huge heavy dark-leaved trees came right down to the sand. Behind, the ground seemed to rise to a low hill. Looking north the slopes of the mountain rose steeply beyond a thick plantation of palms. But the peak, which looked a good 2000 feet up to me, was bare and forbidding.

'It's a volcano. Erupts sometimes! Hence the dark sand,' Peter had shouted as we came past on our way down.

'Not this weekend let's hope!' I shouted back.

Now indeed it did look utterly peaceful, thick with forest on its steep flanks and only a little daunting where the naked rock towered to the final cone. It made a majestic backdrop to the scene, filling the northern sky. I stood for quite a time just taking it all in. How could it have happened? Such an extraordinary skein of coincidences for me to find myself in this marvellous and wildly improbable situation, just because I'd happened to say I'd like to try life on a desert island, 'just to see what it feels like'!

'If you really want to, I can fix it,' Peter had said.

He came out with it quite casually. In fact, thinking it over, the whole thing seemed absolutely casual. And yet, by hindsight, how strange. You never can tell what's round the corner!

I happened to be flying out to Sydney; but when Quantas put down at Bombay there was a signal from the office asking me to reroute myself via Singapore. I'd find details awaiting me at our place there. I'm used to this sort of thing, so I obeyed instructions, did my stuff and, only the same day, got news that the Sydney conference was postponed for a week. That left me with time on my hands so, on the spur of the moment, I decided to sidestep over to Manila. I'd never seen the Philippines, so it would be new, interesting and might turn out to be useful. I booked myself into the Adrian, which the travel agent assured me was a small but exclusive hotel, and there, the evening I arrived, I ran into Peter in the bar.

Since we hadn't seen each other since college days, and that was all of fifteen years before, it was quite a reunion. We'd been pretty close at that time partly because we'd shared digs, but more, I suppose, because we got on, as they say, in some peculiar way. I liked his honesty, his assurance, the way he always seemed to know the answers. He was reading law, while I was struggling with economics. My father, and my grandfather incidentally, were in the Church and it was assumed I'd follow the tradition. But suddenly and strangely I dug my toes in and flatly refused. It must have been instinctive, but at the time I put it down to the influence of my uncle Tom. I idolized him because he said all the practical things I wanted to hear. 'The Church is a calling, my boy,' he boomed, in his no-nonsense way. 'So make damn sure you're called to another world before you opt out of this one.'

So I took his advice and opted for economics. 'Nobody knows what it means, my boy, but it sounds good.' I certainly hadn't any idea what it meant and never did work up much enthusiasm for it. But we didn't take our studies too seriously in those days and, looking back, I suppose they were the happiest days of my life and it was just pressure of circumstances that had let our friendship slip into no more than the usual Christmas card and the futile resolution, 'I must see old

Peter.' But now, meeting up unexpectedly in such different circumstances, after quite some time, all the pleasure we'd found in each other's company came back. It turned out that Peter was running the hotel and a gang of tourists had just booked in, so it was quite late when we sat down to dine together.

As far as I was concerned it turned into a sort of confessional, though I didn't think of it that way at the time. Peter was a good listener and though I hadn't intended to, I found myself talking quite openly, and, I suppose, a bit apologetically about myself. I haven't had a particularly interesting or eventful life. What it added up to was that, through an introduction from uncle Tom to an old chum, high up in United Pesticides, I'd got a job there and, slowly climbing the ladder, there I'd been ever since. 'So, now, believe it or not, I'm the Far Eastern rep of United Pesticides - and that's about it,' I ended, I suppose a bit lamely.

'But that's a success story!' cried Peter. 'Why be apologetic about it?'

'Because . . .' and I remember I paused because I'd kept it all bottled up for years. 'Because my job - selling the things we sell - used to be all right. I mean getting rid of malaria, bilharzia and all sorts of pests that killed people, interfered with food production and all that seemed fine. But it turned out that the things we sold weren't always effective, did damage to wild life, polluted water supplies and so on. So gradually I lost belief in our products. I developed a sort of moral sense about it all. Things were pretty well controlled near home, but abroad, in the Far East, Africa, we're still selling dangerous, toxic drugs.'

'Yes. And I hear you can't win. Nature always finds ways to beat you.'

'Yes. And that's only one aspect of it. I feel it goes deeper than that. It's what I call human paranoia. Only

4

the human race matters. The whole world exists for us, to satisfy our superiority, our greed, our comfort, our satisfaction. I feel that's wrong. Life, nature, belongs to everybody. We ought to serve life, not expect life to serve us . . . Remember those talks we had in the old days about changing things, the purpose of life and all that?'

'Of course.'

'I suppose my background - Dad being in the Church - and, well, I suppose those deeper feelings nobody ever speaks about, over the years they began to stir things up inside me. I began to feel it all wasn't right . . . and yet I'm doing it! Because it's my living, it's all I know how to do - but inside, I'm frustrated. My life's not right - if you see what I mean.'

Peter nodded. 'I see exactly what you mean. If you grow a conscience, everything's a question.'

'Exactly! So I'm looking for answers.'

'Married?'

'Sort of. I'm abroad a good deal and Sybil's taken to living her own life. Can't say I blame her. But you know how it is. No rows; but no relationship really.'

'Kids?'

'No. One of us must be impotent. Me probably!'

Peter was looking at me seriously. 'You used to be so keen, so full of enthusiasm, John. Remember how we were going to change the world? Remember how we despised the lowering of standards, the lack of principles, the all-round permissiveness? I expected to hear that you'd been leading protests, marching with the C.N.D. and all that. Where's it all gone?'

'It's . . . evaporated, I suppose . . .' I remember as I said it, the whole waste of my life came into focus. I felt it as I'd never felt it before and I went on, I suppose a bit emotionally, 'If you hope to keep your job today, Peter, and satisfy your employers, you have to give the

5

right answers, do the right things, live the sort of life that goes down well in the office - and keep anything else to yourself. But it sort of eats you away, saps you inside, deadens everything - you even begin to find yourself acting like the others, thinking like the others ...'

'But could you? Did you?'

'What else could I do? How many people do you know who really love their work? Nowadays you hang on to your job. You're lucky to have one. The best you can hope for is to keep it till you retire.'

'John! You talk like an old man! Have you forgotten how we used to enthuse about taking chances, running risks?'

'I'm beginning to wonder if there's anything worth taking chances for!'

'Of course there is! There are always possibilities, always opportunities.'

'Well, tell me,' I said, for I did feel a bit nettled, 'what chances have you taken? Have you gambled with your life? How did you come to be running this hotel, for instance? What about all the ideals you started out with? Don't be so bloody smug, Peter.'

Peter laughed. 'I must say, when you look back on it, there's really no way of knowing how things will turn out, is there? Luck - or destiny - has its own plans for us. Did I ever tell you my mother was Greek?'

'No.'

'She's got a brother, Kosta, and he happens to be in Consular Service out here and when I came down, Dad thought it would be a good idea if I saw the world. So he gave me a thousand pounds and told me to come home when I'd spent it. In the course of the trip, I turned up here. I liked it very much. You never come to the end of the islands and, when I'd made friends, I spent quite a bit of time sailing around and generally enjoying myself.

I wanted to stay on; but as money was running out that meant finding a job. So I managed to get myself taken on as a waiter at the Royal, learned a bit of the lingo and by pure luck, and Kosta pulling the strings, got the job of assistant manager at this hotel. So then I settled down to work and began to learn the ropes and eventually became the manager of the place. Then it changed hands and I expected to have to move on; but it turned out that the Spanish family who'd bought it, rich people from Mindanao, took a fancy to me and, to cut a long story short, I married Rosa, one of their daughters, and the family made over the hotel to us as a sort of dowry.'

'What wonderful luck!'

'Yes. You know this is a fascinating part of the world. Wonderful hospitality, wonderful generosity. Lots of money about, but also a lot of poverty and simplicity, primitive life. Some of these island tribes are still in the stone age. There are thousand of islands, you know, half of them without names or inhabitants, waiting to be explored. For our honeymoon, Rosa and I sailed round some of them. It was marvellous! Sleep. Dream. Bathe. Fish. The world to ourselves! Of course we were terribly lucky. Rosa's family happens to be in the millionaire class so everything's easy. I could have let go, become a real layabout - nearly did! - but, luckily again, there was the hotel. I found I had an urge to make money, make a profit! Surprising! I don't remember having it in the days when we used to talk . . . But now, I must say I do enjoy making this place top class and making it pay!'

Looking at Peter while he was talking, I began to see how much he'd changed. This was not the Peter of our college days, the Peter I had known. He'd grown, matured, and I felt my old warmth and respect for him increase. After all he'd gone down to the bottom of the ladder and worked his way up. I'd never taken risks like

7

that. It had paid off, seemingly by chance - but was it something more? Was it because he'd done it that things had all turned out so well for him?

Deep in all this, I hardly noticed that he'd stopped talking. His silence brought me back to his face. It seemed different, as if he had gone into another part of himself and his voice, when he spoke, sounded different too.

'But that's only part of my life, John,' he was saying. 'There are curious things going on in this part of the world, strange exciting things I don't really believe in, but . . .'

'Such as?' He was always a great one for secrets.

'You know what you were saying about wasting your life? I've had that feeling too, a need to be involved in something bigger than just my own personal life. When I was in India, swanning around as a tourist, I began to be fascinated by the mosques, the temples, the extraordinary vigour and variety of belief! So many different ways to live, so many different things to believe in! I felt crude. Ignorant. Of course I couldn't identify with those ideas; but I saw that if one could find something . . .'

'Yes! That's it, Peter! That's it! Find something! You know, I'm a very ordinary sort of man, timid I suppose, frightened of taking risks, frightened of people, scared of sex, second rate really . . . But it's a bit like Walter Mitty. There's another side of me that, if it got the chance, I feel could turn out to be a leader, a hero. But it never seems to get that chance. I can't get out of the groove, out of the rat race. I need something to bring me to life, something to live for! What have I got to look forward to? Another twenty years doing what I'm doing now! And then what? Retiring and dying! There's got to be something more to my life than that, Peter, for God's sake!'

8

'Perhaps there could be - if you're lucky ...' He paused, as if he wasn't quite sure whether to go on or not. 'You know, in this half-forgotten corner of the world, there do seem to be things to be found which point the way to something quite, quite different ...'

I felt a little tremor of excitement at the tone of his voice. But he fell silent again, thinking, and somehow I didn't dare interrupt him. But at last, 'Peter,' I said, 'if you'd care to tell me, I'm serious. I'm desperate. I really do want something ... different.'

'Could you cope with the simple life, John?' He was smiling at me rather quizzically. 'I mean we're all pretty well glued to the fleshpots, however idealistic we sound. When it comes to the crunch, can we really give up the comforts of civilization?'

'I've often wondered about that. In principle, of course, I think I could, but it would be useful to have some way of testing oneself, having a trial run, so to speak. To be dumped on a desert island, for instance, and left to fend for oneself, that would be really something.'

It was then Peter made the extraordinary offer that had landed me here.

'If you'd really like to try that, I can fix it.'

CHAPTER TWO

I suppose it must have been late afternoon before I awoke. I'd lugged my pack up into the shade of the trees, pulled out a towel, stripped off and taken a dip in the glorious water. It was a new experience for me to swim in a tropical lagoon. Peter had lent me a mask and snorkel and unveiled the wonders of this underwater world. Through the limpid warmth I could see for ever.

There were coral clumps, some dark brown and dead, rotted away, looking like castle ruins, turreted and spired or gashed into chasms and caves. Others were like living boulders four or five feet across, lapped in yellow velvet, seemingly soft to touch, and upthrust from within them they had nobbly bumps, exactly like the horns of baby deer. I just lay and drifted, gazing at the wonder of this underwater world. The vistas were endless. Glorious. Some coral grew like antlers, many-branched and fierce, some like monster cannon balls were piled on each other, like gigantic sponges. There were even cedar trees, standing on trunks with foliage outspreading in great gorgeous green horizontal fans ...

I, a gawky intruder into all this wonder, lay spellbound over a floor of chestnut brown, the powdered lava from eruptions of a thousand years ago. And on this floor crawled sea slugs, big as Bologna sausages, which I had heard the Chinese chewed to make them strong in love. The porcupiny spikes of sea urchins guarded a hundred caves, cushions as big as footstools, maroon or midnight blue, lay here and there and, decorating every clump, peopling each vista, moving under a thousand ledges and emerging, wary, from a million caves, went the fish, the teeming population of this world ...

At last I came out, drugged by the heat, and then I suppose, what with the excitement of the experience, the beauty of the place, the loneliness, the sweep of the sea and the soft air scented from flowers somewhere nearby, I just dropped off.

There were great galleons of cloud sailing the western horizon when I woke and went to sit on the shore. Far off, the silhouettes of other islands lay like boulders of ebony on the evening sea, now turning gold in the sunset. A shining pathway was laid over the water and above it the clouds turned to spreading shields of molten metal, which faded to glowing copper and darkened in the swift twilight. Before I had properly tasted the wonder of it all, night had come, unsuspected, unbidden, and there was the moon gliding between the branches overhead.

I suppose I was a bit overwhelmed by it all. It was such a new experience, such a complete contrast to the way my life usually is; it was too much. Everything was strange. Warm perfumes drifted by on the air. I could hear the drum beat of the rollers on the reef. Yet I seemed enveloped in absolute silence, embraced by wonder. It seduced me, frightened me. I felt anything could happen. If you knew how to make the magic calls, choirs of whales, schools of dolphins, sea monsters, mermaids, Poseidon himself, they would all materialize to complete the wonder of this life too good to be true.

Then in the mundane way things seem to trip you up at the very gates of heaven, it suddenly struck me that I hadn't eaten anything all day and was hungry! I'd have to dip into my emergency rations. No good starting fishing or hunting at this hour. So I rummaged in my pack, fished out some food and just sat there, blissfully happy, thinking how Peter would have laughed to see me solemnly munching my processed cheese and biscuits in the moonlight.

A few stars seemed larger, brighter than they ought to have been. The moon had set her spinnaker and was sailing serenely through her dark seas. All you could hear was the small talk of the wavelets on the beach and the low boom of the reef. A light breeze, mercifully cool after the heat of the day, set the fronds of some palms talking quietly to one another as they touched. The rest of the world was still, breathing in a wonderful sleep. Everything was silent. Sea, mountains, earth, sky, all silent. This was how it should be. I suddenly saw how the whole world around us lived, grew, multiplied, died, in a thousand different ways - and never a word said!

Then I became aware of a strange disturbance in the water, some way off, near the break in the reef. It was quickly followed by explosive movements and the plunge and rush of dark forms moving quickly and purposefully in my direction. Only fish, big fish, could make such a commotion. Black sword blades cut up through the water and, as they came nearer, I heard the blow and gulp of urgent breathing. Dolphins! It could only be a small school of dolphins out for an evening stroll in the lagoon.

My attention had been so completely absorbed by this sudden moonlight apparition that I did not see the girl till she was in the water. She was running headlong, arms outstretched, calling something, a great cry of welcome, as she plunged towards the fish. Could they have heard, known in some way, that she was coming? They seemed to quieten as they glided nearer. It was all so sudden, so unexpected, that, hardly knowing why, I jumped up and ran down the sand after her. But at the water's edge I stopped. There was no danger. The girl and the big fish seemed to have met to play with one another.

There followed the most magical sight that ever was! The dolphins and the girl were outlined in whorls and streams of phosphorescence. As she flung herself at the nearest fish, seemed to climb onto his back, the sea boiled in swirling eddies of light. The two plunged underwater together. Cascades of light streamed from the fish's tail and from the girl's flying hair. They surfaced in a leap, she still clinging to his back, shouting in a sort of ecstasy, to fall back again into this wild seafire that made every movement a whirl of light glowing from within, always dissolving to reform into new dissolving wonders. Again they plunged and leapt and the great fish seemed airborne for a moment, to fall, crack and splash, back into its element. Then, as suddenly as it had begun, it was over. The fish slid away, their contrails dissolving, and the girl was left standing alone, silhouetted against the water. She stood for some moments gazing after them. Then she turned and saw me.

Naked as the day she was born, this young sea goddess stood for a moment, cleared her throat and spat into the sea. Then, shaking her hair which hung long behind her, she strode through the water towards me, stopped and looked me straight in the eye. Her eyes were really glorious, warm and full of welcome. Then she raised both hands and, as I took them, she gave them a sort of shake. 'Sibu!' she said, dropped them and walked straight past me to the shore and, without looking back, disappeared into the trees.

I stood there, gazing after her, quite bemused by such an extraordinary meeting. The whole thing was unbelievable. Things like this simply don't happen to a travelling salesman on his first visit to a desert island. Besides it was perfectly clear to me that, whatever Peter might have said, this was *not* a desert island.

*

I spread my groundsheet at the foot of a tree close to the shore and sat there in the shadows. They seemed darker for the moonlight that silvered open patches between them. Here night did not seem to be night at all, just a twilight silence before the gasp of a new dawn. To say that I was contented did not really describe my state. I felt extraordinarily alive! The assault on my senses had already been greater than I could have imagined possible. But the peace and beauty of the night did not bring quiet, it brought a strange sense of well being such as I had never known before. Yet the sudden appearance of that girl raised a host of questions. It must mean there were other people on the island, perhaps a community, maybe a hostile community? That, in other circumstances, would have been quite enough to work me up into a state of nervous anxiety, fear even . . . But here none of it seemed to touch me. I felt nothing here would harm me. The island breathed an all-pervasive benevolence.

I folded my towel to make a pillow and lay down to sleep; but just as I was dropping off, I heard the sharp crack of a breaking twig and the rustle of feet on leaves. I sat up quickly to see a child coming confidently towards me, obviously knowing I was there. As that slim figure walked into a patch of moonlight, I saw she wore nothing but a skirt of grasses. There were flowers in her hair and she carried a posy in her hand. She came straight towards me without hesitation and, as she put the posy in my hand, took both my hands in hers, giving me the same greeting as the girl had done in the sea. I had already got to my feet to take her hands. 'Riri!' she smiled gravely and, still holding onto my right hand, turned and gently but firmly started to lead me back through the trees the way she had come.

When she saw I was not reluctant to follow, she stepped out more confidently, looking up at me from time to time and smiling as if to reassure me. The path led slightly uphill and then opened into a small clearing. At one side I could make out the slope of a thatched roof, standing on slender columns with a floor or veranda about a metre above the ground. Seated on the edge of this veranda was an old man, or rather a man whose face was lined, leathery and somewhat severe, but whose body, though filled out and well covered, was still young. The shoulders were heavy, muscular, the torso broad, the thighs strong and fully rounded. As he rose to greet me he gave the impression of a strong man in the prime of life. Like the others he took both my hands and shook them firmly, bowing slightly. 'Roka!' He gave me a cautious smile. I returned this equally cautiously, on guard at meeting a stranger and particularly a dark massive stranger, on a supposedly desert island, lost God knows where in the Philippines!

I managed 'Good evening. How kind of you to make me welcome,' - or something inane like that before I petered out; to which my host (for this I assumed him to be) made no reply. His face, grown grave again, beckoned forward a woman of about his own age who, smiling broadly, went through the same double handshake routine. 'Pili!' she grinned. Big teeth smiled in her open face and an air of benevolence radiated from that motherly body, whose eyes, even in the moonlight, sparkled warmly. She half led, half shoved me towards a sort of stool of plaited reeds and sat me down on it, while the man, with no apparent effort, swung out a massive tree stump before me. Evidently I was going to be served with food.

All this was strange enough, but before I could make the usual protestations about it all being too good of them and that I really couldn't accept, etc., etc. - which they obviously wouldn't understand anyway - I was cut short by the strangest, most unexpected interruption.

The man, his wife - for this I assumed her to be - the child and the dolphin girl, who emerged at that moment from the shadows bringing food, all together, as if it was something usual, habitual, broke into a quiet low humming.

It was so spontaneous, harmonious and free from any taint of affectation that it stopped me in mid-thought as it were. Listening to this strange music, which continued all through the meal, brought a sense of ritual to everything they did. Yet it was perfectly ordinary. The child first offered me a small piece of the root of some herb and signalled me to eat it. The taste was somewhat bitter but I swallowed it reluctantly, imagining it to must be some aid to digestion or an aperient or something. Meanwhile her sister was offering me fish carefully laid out on a dish of leaves. It was cut up, raw, and she motioned me to dip pieces of it into a shell she was holding in her other hand. This turned out to be sea water which, to my surprise, set off the taste of the fish to perfection. When I had finished this, I saw that the child was cutting open some large fruit, rather like a melon. She offered me pieces to eat. It was sweet and full of flavour.

Throughout the meal the elderly people sat quietly, absorbed in their music and I felt I had never been such an honoured guest in my life, with those two dark girls kneeling either side of me, their bent heads crowned with flowers. Even when the meal was over this improvization of harmony continued, soothing, gentle and, I am sure, a wonderful aid to the digestion! The whole thing had put me into a sort of trance, unexpected and perfect and somehow, I didn't exactly know how, I felt I had come to rest here.

Then, abruptly, the humming stopped. The girls got up. Things were carried away. I too rose, bowed and made a gesture of thanks to my hosts. I pointed to the beach and made to withdraw. But immediately Pili stopped me and, with an imperious gesture, flung an arm round my shoulders and propelled me towards the veranda. There was evidently no doubt as to where I should sleep. I climbed onto the floor, rather sheepishly, I suppose, not being used to a communal bed. But I was by now so tired I would have slept anywhere. So I stretched out on one of the mats and the child, who always seemed to turn up at the right moment, put a pillow of sweet scented leaves under my head. Taking another for herself, she lay down with her back to me and feeling for my hand, confidently drew it over her side as if for protection. This was at once so endearing yet so natural, I felt perfectly at ease and, as I drifted off, felt the other girl's arm steal over my side to hold me. So, sandwiched between the two girls I slept. I suppose it was about as near to the Garden of Eden as I was ever likely to get.

I woke next morning to a dawn of such lucid splendour it felt as if sun, sea and sky had never met before. At first I couldn't remember where I was; but it didn't seem to matter and I stretched luxuriously, coming to. Then I looked round and saw that I was alone; for the others the day had already begun. My first thought was of the sea, so I ran down to the shore to find the whole family already in the water. The old people were out on the reef which, at that particular state of the tide, appeared to be just awash. They were bending down, busy collecting something. The child, in the shallows, diving between the coral heads, had just come up with a large disgusting sea slug which she proudly displayed for my inspection. From the delight with which she held it up it was evidently a delicacy.

The girl was swimming back from the reef carrying in her teeth a net bag containing shells which the others had gathered. She dumped these under the shade of a tree and strode back to the water with the empty net in her hand, making gestures for me to join her. Tall, slim and wonderfully made, I thought she looked just as much a sea goddess as when I had first seen her - could it be only the night before? I plunged into the sea after her, but she easily outdistanced me in our race for the reef.

For me to stand on a coral reef was a sort of dream come true, tropical lagoons and pirates having been one of my childhood fantasies. But the great submerged wall of rock was nothing like my dream of it. It was a broad highway, foaming with water and pitted with innumerable pockets and crevices, the refuge and habitat of all manner of small sea creatures, shellfish, prawns, crabs, anemones, tiny fish, all surviving and seemingly quite at home under the crashing weight of the surf, which day and night broke over them. The great rollers eternally attacking the barrier, rose in their splendour, curling before they broke to display large fish as if crystallized in the clear water. Somehow avoiding the curling roar that would destroy them, they sank back as the waves broke, only to reappear again flashing silver in the one that followed.

I walked ankle deep in foam, feeling the reef tremble under the weight of the seas, the spray splashing over me and the warmth of the early morning sun bringing a glow to my skin. I suppose I had never felt so alive before, snatched out of my years of routine and suddenly set free. The girl gave me another bag of shells to take back to the shore. I swam back and, as I walked up onto the sand, stopped, suddenly overwhelmed by it all.

I had come here, expecting to face the challenge of fending for myself on a desert island and, almost at once had been swept into situations so strange and magical I could hardly believe them. That girl, playing with the dolphins, it was unbelievable. Why had they come? Did she call them? They say some people can. And then that supper! The weird crooning music, the beautiful food, the hospitality, the feeling of being accepted, at home, how could such things have happened to me? Was Peter's plane a sort of passport to anyone who came in it? Was he playing some sort of a joke on me to see how I would react? Were there other families on the island, some sort of community? The whole thing was full of questions. But I suddenly felt it didn't matter. I didn't care. It was all magical. I found myself laughing for no reason and looked round to see the old people and the girls all following me ashore. We walked up the hill to their house.

There was a small fire smoking nearby and this they quickly fanned into flame. We were evidently going to eat the shells now, at once. They seemed quite excited about it and the old people rubbed each other's cheeks and kissed. Quite sexy! At breakfast time! I couldn't think why. The shells were very beautiful, like large winkles, about the size of pigeon's eggs, mottled in shades of beige and pink. They sizzled and cracked with a loud report and were raked out, broken and the flesh shared between us. Even I, with all my nervousness about strange food, once I'd tried them had to agree they were delicious. A second and a third round were cooked and eaten amid rising excitement and laughter. What was it all about? Offering me the contents of a shell, the third time around, the girl, Sibu, deliberately came close and rubbed herself against me. I stepped back, of course, laughing, I suppose a bit sheepishly. The old people seemed to find this hilarious.

I've never thought of myself as prudish; but my upbringing in a clergyman's family, had, I suppose been rather straitlaced and 'proper'. My father talked a lot about sin and especially sexual sin. But nobody told me the facts of life. So I kept clear of girls up at college and when I did take one girl out, I found I had no wish to touch or kiss her. Was it that I was terrified of the whole thing, scared of my own body? I never analysed it. I just shut it out of my life.

That was the trouble between me and Sybil. I didn't want to confess it to Peter when he asked me, but it was the physical side of our marriage that had gone wrong. I'd really loved Sybil and though I was nervous about marriage, I thought that when it was all legal and there was no sense of shame or hurry, it would be all right. But on our wedding night I simply couldn't do anything. I made excuses of course, said I was too excited, too tired and so on; but I never did consummate the marriage. Sybil couldn't understand it. She even thought it must be her fault. I couldn't understand it either; but there it was. I felt nothing. I told her I thought I must be frigid, there must be something wrong with me, but I was sure it would all come right. So, because she was a decent girl and because she knew I had really loved her at the beginning, she put up with it for a time; but it got no better and our marriage inevitably petered out and I couldn't do anything about it.

Up to that moment I had been enjoying everything I had shared with this strange family. It was their innocence, their purity that attracted me. But now suddenly everything was different. It had simply never occurred to me that the shells were a powerful aphrodisiac. That sort of thing belonged to a rather indecent world I knew nothing about. To need artificial stimulus to excite normal feelings seemed to me to be decadent. In any case the shells had had no such effect on me. So when, a moment later, I saw Roka swing his wife off her feet, which considering her weight was no mean feat, and lay her wide-legged on the ground to mount her with obvious relish, I was dumbfounded. I didn't know where to look.

Then from the way Sibu looked at me, I suddenly saw she expected to do the same thing. Without thinking about it, I just took to my heels and made a dash for the beach. I didn't know what I was doing. I didn't think. I just wanted to get away. But when I heard her behind me, knew she was catching me up, and when she finally tackled me and we both came to the ground with a thud, it flashed through my mind that she was a wild savage and I should probably have to fight for my life.

Somehow she got on top of me and I turned on my back, fighting her off; but she was very strong, seized both my arms, straddled me and in that position we, so to speak, came to, breathing hard, glaring at each other. Now what?

After a long moment it seemed everything grew quiet, different. There was no fury in her eyes, only a sort of warm sexual expectation. She leaned forward over me and I slowly became aware of her body, of her marvellous warm, sensual and exciting scent, intoxicating me, making me forget everything else. For a long moment she remained so, as if to envelop me in desire, eating me with her eyes, mesmerizing me.

Something was happening. Something that had never happened to me before, as if I had just woken up to myself. I felt my manhood making demands she was eager to accept and the whole encounter slowly grew, threatened like a thunderstorm, to burst in a lightning flash over both of us and die out to a still, deep-breathing calm. I lay still. It was as if I had been reborn. I had lost my fears, my feeling of giving way to my lower nature. It was glorious! Now I knew what it was to be fulfilled in the needs of the body.

CHAPTER THREE

I have put down just what happened on the evening and the following morning after my arrival on the island. But, on reflection it seems to me that perhaps such an opening may give a false impression. Tropical islands and coral reefs have become a sort of package tour cliché for dreams, indolence and lovemaking, and indeed the island offered all these soporifics and more. But, in fact, the way people lived there was quite different from this fantasy of it. Ritual, custom and strange influences had evolved in an original and striking way.

The first signs of these showed in their devotion to cleanliness. That morning, after we had recovered, Sibu at once led me to a pool beyond the house where spring water poured in through a bamboo pipe. Here she picked up a sponge and washed herself thoroughly. I followed suit. She then rinsed out her mouth and evidently expected me to do the same. Meanwhile Riri had wrung out my bathing trunks and gave them to me. I suppose in such a climate to keep their bodies sweet and clean, such habits came naturally. The smell of my sweat-soaked shirts and shorts disgusted them. Their scanty clothes, when they wore any, were like the flowers they put in their hair, just decorations, expressions of gaiety or happiness. Nakedness was everyday wear and soon became so to me. The climate laughed at modesty.

Then, dismissing me in a friendly, but practical, offhand sort of way, Sibu pointed to Riri who had evidently been appointed to look after me and the child immediately took my hand and began to lead me off towards the crest of the hill.

Treating what had been for me a wonderful sudden intimacy in such a matter of fact way surprised and shocked me. Did it mean nothing to the girl? Was it just instinct? Was she, like an animal, driven by compulsive desires, forgotten as soon as satisfied? It certainly put new values on sex. Many men would be glad to be rid of the pretences with which it is always surrounded. But to admit it . . .

I was brought out of all this by the child tugging at my hand. I went with her willingly enough for she was an entertaining little guide, gathering flowers for me to smell and then put in her hair, choosing others to put behind my ear, carefully keeping in the shade. We passed open small houses dotted about here and there under the trees and although people could occasionally be seen working around them, they all had a rather preoccupied air, not in the least curious, just pausing to give us a friendly wave as we passed, as if they knew all about me - but how, I wondered? - and did not want to be interrupted. I got the impression that the cool morning hours were the time devoted to work. But it was more than this. Later, when I got to know them better, I found this to be one of their very special virtues, they were always busy. They never hurried, but they never stopped and this general activity seemed to create an air of wellbeing and contentment.

From time to time as we walked I heard the sound of drums, sometimes nearby, sometimes far away. They seemed to speak and answer one another. It wasn't until a later visit that I learned that everything that happened on the island was made common knowledge in this way. It explained why they weren't at all surprised when they saw me and of course they used the drums to call for help, warn of dangers, accidents - or just gossip. But I thought it might take a lifetime to understand them.

When at last we reached the top of the hill and looked over to the east, the prospect was exhilarating. The morning sun glistened on a glittering sea. On our right was a crescent of reef that had formed a low island, protecting a stretch of water between it and the shore. It made a sort of diminutive estuary which narrowed to an inlet where it looked as if some stream came down from the hill behind it. The summit of this hill was in turn outlined against the steeper and more forbidding line of the central mountain which dominated the island.

The ground fell away at our feet towards the estuary and was terraced and green with what I took to be rice fields. People were working in them and the whole scene had an intimate, pastoral feeling about it, quite different from the lagoon and the long open shore where we had landed.

I stood there for some time, enchanted by the view. The water in the estuary must have been quite shallow for I could see a number of poles sticking up through the surface, some topped with little flags, but the purpose of these I could not at that time determine.

The child drew my attention to some canoes lying out to seaward beyond the end of the reef and pointed to clusters of people, some on the island, some on the shore, all of them looking out to sea and watching the approach of two canoes. These drifted in slowly, occasionally splashing the water with the flats of their paddles in a desultory sort of way. As they came into the estuary, Riri began to get quite excited and kept pointing down at the water, evidently delighted at what she saw there. At first I could see nothing but at length as they came in I thought I could detect a shadow beneath the surface. Meanwhile the men and women who had been waiting for the canoes to arrive slipped quietly and unobtrusively into the water, forming an open line across the estuary. They then began striking the surface of the water with their hands, shouting as they did so. They were skilfully driving a shoal of fish towards the narrows where nets were stretched underwater between the poles on which I had noticed the flags.

We hurried down the hill to see the catch. As the men in the water picked up the flagged poles and drew them together, closing the nets in which the fish were trapped, the whole company burst into song! If the quiet humming of the little family at supper the evening before had surprised me, this chorus of voices, so evidently rejoicing at the happy outcome of their work, astonished me even more. It seemed they were giving vent to their common feelings in a perfectly natural way, yet one which, though I might have felt it inwardly, I could never express like that. It gave me the sense of touching a way of life quite strange to me, exciting and exhilarating.

Quite a large shoal of some thousands of pale, white fish, about the size of herrings, were swimming about peacefully enough in the trap and, from the way the people around were pointing and exclaiming it was clear they were delighted at this living larder. Some with handnets were already taking fish out. Nobody seemed to 'own' the fish. It was evidently a communal undertaking in which everyone shared.

As we stood, a little to one side, watching these people looking at the fish and then striding up out of the water, I was able to get some general idea of what they were like. Obviously it was an established community and Peter knew perfectly well what he was doing in giving me the chance to share in their way of life. On the whole they were lightweight people, spare of figure and small boned. The women in most cases were quite short in stature. Their colouring varied from the dusky velvet of Arabia to the pale coffee of India; but their features were fine, their expressions open, their eyes eloquent. The general impression was of a happy, relaxed people quite free from that half hidden veil of anxiety which seems a general disease in the West.

To them, I must have seemed strange, with my pale, sickly-looking white skin and I suppose my size, bigger and heavier than theirs, must have made me almost a monstrosity. But they were evidently curious about me. Those nearest came up to me and greeted me with the same double handshake, looking me straight in the eyes, giving me their names and smiling. They wanted to touch my white skin and smell me. My smell was clearly important to them and though I felt it was a little strange, I soon accepted it as one of their ways of getting to know me. In the West our senses of taste and smell are so little used they have almost been forgotten. We never wonder if our friends smell good or bad, the odour of our bodies being something into which it would often be indelicate to enquire.

All these good people seemed to accept me and I had a feeling of friendliness and warmth towards them though I could not have said why. None of them attempted to enter into any conversation with me and I assumed they understood we could never communicate that way. Yet their silence didn't seem to separate us. It was even a sort of bond between us. I felt they had no need of conversation. We understand each other, their faces seemed to say, no need to talk.

But all this, so new to me, was again interrupted by a childish tug that insisted we get on with the guided tour and Riri led me away from the sea. Along a stream emerging from the trees, a series of pools had been made, widening out the banks and here people were washing themselves. It seemed to me that, on the whole, they were of exceptional physical beauty, not only their features, but their open fearless expressions and the way men and women mixed in a perfectly natural way. All this, set in a tropical paradise of sun and shade, was so strange and beautiful and carefree, I was wholly entranced by the scene and had a recurrent feeling of joy and liberation such as I had never known before.

Evidently preparations were going forward for some festival and in an open space above the stream, many young men were engaged in practising sports of skill or strength. Running, jumping, wrestling or hurling heavy stones, they were quite unaffected by the heat that was too much for me. I retired to a deep patch of shade to watch their work.

Only one party of girls was left. They were practising a dance which, from the way they kept stopping and going over the same sequence, seemed to be rather difficult and complicated. I certainly could not follow it. They were copying a leader who stood in front of them. At one side two girls were keeping the time on small hollow gourds. I was struck by the serious expression on the faces of these dancers and the concentration they brought to the work and would have been content to go on watching them for some time, but the child evidently thought I had rested enough, pulled me to my feet and we continued upstream.

A short steep rise brought us to the last pool. On its far side stood a bare rock face where the hill above seemed to have been cut off sheer. But the strange thing about this rock was the opening in it. It was a dark archway, which seemed to lead into the heart of the mountain. The stream had been dammed to become a small lake which extended into the darkness. There was something mysterious about it. It certainly gave the child the shivers for she began making strange flapping movements with her arms and uttering little squeaks. I understood that clouds of birds - or could it be bats? - poured through the opening. But when, why? It was all very strange.

At that moment there was a shout and I turned to see two lads I had seen practising below hauling a canoe out of the bushes that lined the far side of the pool. They threw it into the water and made signs to me to join them. Evidently they wanted to show me what lay beyond the archway.

While the boys steadied the canoe, which was pretty small and narrow, I climbed in. One boy took a paddle and jumped into the stern, while the other boy sat in the bows. We paddled briskly to the entrance. The canoe was just a hollowed out tree trunk, very unstable and we were only saved from capsizing by the outriggers, lashed some six feet out from the hull on either side. A few strong strokes headed us for the opening and a moment later we shot through into the unknown!

I do not know what I had expected but it was certainly not this huge cathedral-like cavern that stretched out into the gloom before us. Once inside, the boys lay on their paddles and drifted, looking up, as I did. The sunlight glaring down on the pool outside was reflected, mirroring the curve of the arched entrance to make a sort of dragon's mouth. Above, the roof of the cave lay in twilight which faded into the depths where it seemed to melt into the darkness of the underworld. When one of the boys shouted the sound echoed away into silence and I found myself holding my breath waiting for I knew not what to happen.

We drifted on, the boys as much as I quieted and overawed by this other world, so close to their own, reached through a mere doorway, yet as strange and daunting as crossing from life into death, and as sudden maybe. As we drifted further into the depths, the light became dimmer and the entrance no more than a white circle in a blackness which seemed to crowd closer about us. Absolute, breathless silence reigned, as if another world lived within the world outside, just as close and just as strange. We sat there, silent, listening, alert to life, as if its nature could be grasped and known, as if by separating from it we could find it, by leaving it, possess it.

We were coming back slowly towards the entrance when one of the boys - I suppose to him it was a sort of joke - made a long, high-pitched whistle. Its effect was electrical. The whole roof of the cave was alive with bats and his whistle was evidently an alarm signal of mortal danger. The entire population took to the air! The cave was alive with the beating wings of thousands of hysterical screaming bats! They swarmed about us, missing us by inches. Their thin whistles, their black shadowy wings, chattering teeth and glittering eyes were full of menace. Above all their horrible, all pervading stench filled the air as they wheeled about us. I crouched in the canoe. 'Let's get out of this!' I shouted. Thankfully I felt the canoe move under us and a moment later we emerged into the blessed light of day.

The boys were laughing at the joke they had played on me as they put me ashore, hauled out the canoe and then, without a word or a backward glance, ran off down the hill. But Riri's delight at seeing me safe and sound was plain. The cave terrified her and she seemed to think she had lost me forever, kissed my hands, hid her face against my thigh so affectionately and tenderly that - devoutly glad to be out of the place myself - I lifted her up and kissed her on both cheeks, which she seemed to take as a deserved reward.

By now the heat of the sun was heavy as we left the shade of the trees around the cave pool and continued, taking a pathway towards the base of the small hill on our right. It led to a sort of amphitheatre, a cleft in the hill's side, backed by trees. Towards these the ground sloped slightly upward. It was open, carefully tended and clearly planned to show off its centrepiece, a group of statuary so striking, so strange and unexpected, I stopped, amazed.

Five life-sized figures, closely grouped, were bending towards each other and examining something on the ground between them. They had an air of bewilderment mixed with curiosity and the thing they were looking at was a small golden sphere no bigger than a football. As I walked towards them, fascinated, I saw that these figures were all grotesques, caricatures, made out of straw. But they were no rough effigies, scarecrows to amuse or warn, they were fashioned with great skill. Originally they had evidently been lightly plastered, but now much of the plaster had been washed away, exposing the reeds, which were carefully bound together with cords. All this was strange enough, but what riveted the attention was the expression and masterly art in the pose which each of the five figures assumed.

One was all eyes, gazing rapt at the sphere below him, another was all ears, head turned sideways, intently listening, a third was stooped, nose pointed as if inhaling, a fourth gaped, tongue hanging out, while the fifth, arms and hands extended, stretched forward eagerly, trying to touch the sphere to know what it might mean. It was the intensity of their attention that amazed me. Life depended, so it seemed, on what they could understand.

I was so concentrated on this that I had made my way right round the group before I noticed Riri. Evidently to her these grotesques were very funny. She was miming their postures to the life - and I could not help noticing how perfectly she did it - staring, putting out her tongue, gazing at the imaginary ball - she did it all expertly as if she had been trained to it and laughed,

30

looking at me for approval. I laughed with her, but I was still riveted by the bizarre, enigmatic air of those posturing creatures. What did they mean? What were they trying to say? Impossible that they should have been created just for amusement.

My head was full of questions as we walked on. Apart from the strange feeling that I got from that group, there was the riddle of the technique. How had such things been fashioned from grass and string, for that was what it amounted to? These were strange skills - not the work of simple people. And why would they create things like this knowing they could not last, knowing they would be washed away by a few storms? I could not make it out.

So, reluctantly, quite lost in my own thoughts, I let Riri lead me further along the path. We came to a carefully tended plantation of palms.

CHAPTER FOUR

The tall palms stood in order, like columns holding up the sky. The ground was open beneath their grey elegant trunks. Here there was an almost churchlike feeling of silence and peace. But I was far away, pre-occupied, still puzzling about those five figures. What were they trying to tell me? One was speaking, surely, but another listening, a third trying to smell, a fourth to touch - the senses! They must be the senses! Then what was that yellow ball? Why did it mesmerize them so? What did it tell them?

I was jerked out of this reverie by a sudden shout almost from overhead. It came from a tiny dark figure crouching right up under the head of a palm. A small boy was making signals to us and a second later down, with a heavy thump, pretty well at our feet, dropped a coconut. Then this child, a boy not more than eight years old, clasping hands round the trunk, began, as it were, to walk down the trunk with the agility of an acro-bat. He leapt to the ground, threw an arm round Riri's shoulder, greeted me with the usual two-handed gesture, 'Toni', split open the nut and handed it to us to drink. I was surprised to find how cool and refreshing it was.

So we sat together at the foot of one of the palms. To appear friendly and get on better terms with these two children, I started to ask questions. How old were they? Did they go to school? Where was the boy's house? And so on. I did not expect any answers, but I did expect some sort of a reaction. A few impossible words would

32

come rushing out, we should all laugh. There would have been an exchange and we should all feel silly and friendly and closer to one another.

But nothing of the kind happened. The two children looked at me, smiling gravely, as if they had not heard me, as if they did not know what words were. Their faces were absolutely blank. I felt, in some way, alarmed at their silence. They suddenly seemed remote, as if they belonged to another race - which indeed they did - but I felt shut out, put in my place. I didn't know how to behave with these children.

Suddenly Toni leant towards Riri and gravely mimicking my way of turning my head and speaking, made some unintelligible noises to her, which passed for words. She at once imitated him perfectly. Then they looked at each other and burst into peals of laughter. Their imitation speech was the funniest thing for years. They laughed and laughed.

I must say I didn't know how to take it. There was something mysterious about it, even frightening. Why did they find my speaking so funny, so ridiculous? Now they had collected themselves, they sat up. They were friends. They were holding hands, saying goodbye. Then suddenly, without a word, the boy jumped to his feet and, with a wave of his hand, ran off through the palms. Riri looked after him with admiration ... but there was something puzzling, something I did not understand. All the people I had met on the island were lively, intelligent, normal in every way - so it appeared. Then what was it that cut them off?

And then I suddenly saw it! And what I saw was so extraordinary, so unbelievable that I couldn't imagine it even. It stopped me dead in my tracks. These people never seemed to speak. They never chatted or passed the time of day. Come to think of it, I had never heard them shout a question, a greeting or a warning. They seemed to have no speech except their names. But that was impossible. How could they communicate? Impossible for people to live together without talking, without speech. Impossible.

And yet they seemed to understand one another. They seemed to know what you wanted before you asked. How did little Riri know she was to take me for a walk, show me the island, look after me, as if I was a tourist? Why? Because of Peter? But Peter said he was dropping me off on a desert island. Did he know it was like this? Did he know the place was inhabited? Or, for some reason, did he want me to find out about it all for myself? I was baffled.

They could smile, they could laugh, they could create those wonderful figures, they could make beautiful music - how could I ever forget that humming while the girls were giving me supper last night? And yet - they could not, or did not want, or had never been taught, to talk to each other, to communicate as the rest of the world did, by speech. Perhaps they didn't need it? Perhaps they had gone beyond it?

Up to that moment I had thought of my desert island weekend as a wonderful escape to Cloud Nine; but now I was beginning to get other ideas, other feelings of quite a different kind. The island was full of overtones, full of questions. That extraordinary group of straw grotesques, who had created them, what were they trying to say? Were they just asking questions? To make people think? But to do that, to create symbols, myths, this was the highest form of art. To find that sort of thing here . . . It was an enigma.

So, deep in these thoughts, I followed Riri, feeling quite alien. I had the sense of another life going on about me, a happy life, a full life, yet strangely different. How I couldn't say. But I felt curious about it all. I wanted to find out. How did these people live? Was there a chief? Elders? Clans? Now suddenly everything seemed to have new roots, new motives, new needs.

We had turned inland from the plantation and, rounding the shoulder of the hill, came in sight of a narrow valley, almost a dell, lying between the hill on one side and the towering slopes of the peak on the other. Its sudden appearance had a breathtaking effect. The scale was just right, depth, breadth and length, the closed vista at the far end, the shape of the woods that bordered it on both sides and the grassy hollow that floored it all. But what caught the eye, causing a sudden ejaculation of delight, were the little pavilions that seemed to float like jewels among the trees down each side of the dell. They gave it all a sort of perfection, a moment caught for ever, like a bee in amber.

These little pavilions were different from all the others I had seen on the island, as if they had some special place and had been set in this idyllic grove for some special reason. The roofs had a secret oriental air, uptilted as if they were smiling. The slender columns that supported them were carved with tiny figures, which made them look like totem poles, but when we came nearer I saw that the creatures they portrayed were simply babies! Dozens of chubby, tubby, smiling babies sat on each other's heads supporting the roofs of these pavilions. The dark wood of which they were made was polished by the touch of many hands. These places must be deeply loved.

Were they the homes of princes, the rulers of the island? Was this a sort of millionaires row? Whatever they were, the thing that made them special was the hangings that made their walls. None of the dwellings I had seen so far were anything more than a roof held up over a floor, open to the winds and eyes of all the world; but these had screens, wall hangings, curtains which, at will, gave complete privacy, or raised, rolled up or pulled aside, invited visitors. The hangings seemed to be made up of a patchwork of bright colours, scalding reds, cool blues, mauves, whites, with accents of black and green and the whole, swinging in the breeze, combined to give the dell a gay, harmonious air, lovely, carefree and yet secure, held in the cup of the little valley.

There were ten of these little palaces, each different from the next owing to the very individual draping of the walls, but together they made a perfect whole. This was added to - as I have so far omitted to say, owing to my preoccupation with the style and setting of the little places - by the dozens of people clustered about each. Some sitting, some arriving with food or flowers, baskets of fruit, lengths of cloth thrown over the shoulders or wound like turbans round their heads. It all made an enchanting scene.

Evidently the little valley was the focus of daily life on the island. But why? I wondered. I had not noticed people coming and going round the other houses we had passed. Riri, as if in answer to my unspoken question (Did she know my thoughts? I was beginning to ask myself.), led me towards the nearest pavilion where we went through the ceremony of the double handshake, the smile, the penetrating look in the eyes, the name, with some fifteen people. I was beginning to know how to comport myself in these encounters, trying to match the warmth of their welcome, but never feeling myself to be sincere enough; but that was quickly forgotten when Riri led me to the central figure, the recipient of all this evident love and devotion.

She was a most beautiful young woman, bearing in her arms a male child a few weeks old. The mother held the infant out to me with such a gesture of pride and love that I was quite overwhelmed. I think she expected me to take the child in my arms, but I am terrified of babies for fear of dropping them, so the best I could do

36

was to take the child's two tiny hands in my own and say my name. At this the newcomer returned me such a look of wisdom, purity and wonder that suddenly tears welled up in my eyes, knowing in that moment for certain, that this young soul had not yet been cut from the celestial regions from which it had come and was telling me, if I could pause to understand, that another sort of life was possible for the pure in heart.

My unexpected tears affected everyone deeply, and immediately turning to it as we might to prayer, a chant, I suppose well known to them, of love and gratitude, stole out onto the air humbly and gently like a thanksgiving to whatever god they believed in. I have to confess I was carried away. I had never heard anything like it in my life. The domestic humming of the night before had touched me by its warmth and intimacy, but this music! These people, who grew stranger and stranger to me by the minute, were masters of sound. They loved it for the sound's sake, to make it out of their own throats, to harmonize it with others, to achieve out of its melting qualities the whole gamut of the joy and sorrow in the human condition. To me it brought a new dimension to music. No words were necessary to pass on the feelings it wanted to share. No instruments either. What squealing of catgut or bellowing of brass could compare with the infinite range and subtlety of the human voice?

As this music ended like a benediction, a silence fell on all of us and I felt I was being offered, if I dared to take it, the love and acceptance of the whole community. It was broken by the little nutbrown lump that had been the cause of it all, kicking sturdy brown legs and demanding food. At this everyone laughed and one or two of the men took off their wreaths of flowers and put them round my neck. Feeling overcome with emotion and the dizzy scent of the blossoms, I stood there stupidly not knowing what to do, till Riri caught hold of my hand and saved the situation by slowly leading me away.

We walked on down the dell. At each pavilion it was the same. The centre of attraction was the infant. Boys or girls, they were all about the same age and must have been born within a few days of each other. Was this little valley a sort of lying-in ward for young mothers? Who were the husbands? At each pavilion there seemed to be half a dozen men who could have qualified for the honour. Besides them there were many friends young and old and much coming and going between the little places. It all seemed like a family party with everybody blissfully happy. Yet, except for an occasional complaint from one of the children or the brooding outbreak of that low humming that seemed to accompany their moods, there was hardly a sound.

While I was gradually becoming reconciled to the idea that these people did not speak, in the usual sense of the word, that is they did not use language to pass their thoughts, it was far from being a silent community. Earlier, as I was walking with Riri, I had heard occasional sudden ejaculations, cries, coming from here and there, without apparent reason, but there was so much to see, I had paid it no particular attention. But now, looking at the busy scene round the pavilions, I began to notice how they all seemed to have a way of emitting a sort of cry in moments of pleasure, surprise or anxiety. And often, thinking it over afterwards, I likened it to the birdsong one may hear on a summer morning. Each voice seemed to have its own character and later on I was able to recognize each one by his or her personal cry. These cries were sometimes very beautiful in themselves, just as the song of a thrush or a nightingale is beautiful. And as, in nature there are times when the whole world is silent and others when it comes alive with all sorts of sounds, so here there were times of silence and others when the air was sweet with these sudden phrases of song that jumped from people's hearts just, it seemed, for the pleasure of making them.

Yet something more seemed to pass between them than these occasional cries and their silences gave an air of dignity and contentment to all they did. It was so different from the obsessive need we have to make a lot of noise about everything we do. Here nothing was drowned in speech and I began to see all the things I usually missed by labelling them with words. A whole area of experience I had passed by, taken for granted, came rushing into life. I felt movements, colours, scents and sounds, with which nature all the time flooded our senses coming into miraculous focus. In a hundred ways I came alive and had the sense of being born into another world.

After dozens of greetings and double handshakes, we retraced our way back up the dell just as a thunder shower broke over us. We ran for cover to the nearest pavilion, glad to accept the shelter of their roof. Here the atmosphere was now quite different. It seemed to be a time for siesta. People were lying down, often in each others arms, as relaxed and content as animals. In one corner, to my intense surprise (and I must add, embarrassment), was a couple making love. They were surrounded by friends of both sexes who, with much crooning and stroking and loving encouragement seemed to be doing everything possible to increase their delight in it. When it had come to an end they all lay there together and slept in great content. Why, I began to ask myself, had this, the most beautiful and intimate of human relationships, always been branded as secret, even sinful? Never seen, as it certainly was here, to be a celebration of creation in which others could share.

When at last we took our leave of these good people,

Riri led me back down to the long curving sable beach where we had first landed. The tide was out and a swathe of sand lay along the water's edge. Suddenly, I don't know why, I stopped and burst out laughing. It was the result, I suppose, of the wealth of new impressions that had flooded over me ever since I had been on the island. They were all so unexpected, so new, healthy and exciting - and yet so warm and full of love - it left me with a mixed up sensation of bewilderment and wonder and I suppose the only thing I could do about it was laugh!

I looked at little Riri and then, just out of high spirits, I started to dance! It was no more than a jig, waving my arms about, snapping my fingers, crossing one foot over the other and turning round, the sort of thing you do when you hear some tune on the radio and want to let off steam.

Without a second's hesitation Riri joined me. She copied my movements, turned around, snapped her little fingers and then, as a sort of excitement started to take hold of us both, began to improve on my steps till I found myself following her and together we improvised what seemed to me then the most wonderful dance I had ever danced in my life. I daresay it would have looked comical to onlookers had there been any, but there weren't. There was just the long curve of the beach with the sunset for a backdrop and two happy figures, one too big and one too small, whirling round each other, carried away with the joy of just being alive!

CHAPTER FIVE

I woke next morning to find the little house deserted. I had overslept. But near my mat was fruit. Some bananas and a papaya - and the usual small piece of root. I chewed this thoughtfully, smiling at the way little Riri seemed to think it her duty to look after me - although I still hadn't the least idea what this ritual chewing was about. I had a dip in the sea and came up to splash myself all over with fresh water from the pool. But all the time my head was simply teeming with all the strange things that had happened to me the day before. For strange they were, after all.

The way that Sibu had captivated me and wakened my body to a sort of ecstasy, that alone was a miracle, more than enough for me for one day and many days to come! And then, in the afternoon, the way those young people had made their lovemaking a social affair, enjoying it all together. It ought to have shocked me; but strangely enough again, here, it didn't. I had been brought up to think of sex as something never to be spoken about. Birth was almost an immaculate conception! People conspired to ignore the miraculous, wonderful part of it. But here it was all part of life. I felt that was healthy, right.

And then I remembered hearing about something in Captain Cook's journals, how on arriving at Tahiti, he and his officers were invited to witness after dinner displays of lovemaking in which young people were encouraged to learn how to show off their talents and skills - at which arts, he wryly remarked, they did not seem to stand in much need of tuition. The Captain, a most humane and liberal-minded man, far in advance of the accepted moralities of his time, himself reflected on the question in his diaries. Why was the sexual act considered sinful?

But that was only part of my day. There were lots of other things, just as strange - those ghastly bats and that very odd group of figures gazing at that little golden ball, the feeling of joy that suffused the dell where all those young mothers were feeding their babies. Everything in the day seemed to have been washed over with a feeling of happiness. These people were in such a wonderful state. Was it that which gave the sense of liberation, of elation? Maybe it would wear off, but now while it lasted, it was wonderful, simply wonderful!

And beyond all that was the feeling of being accepted, being perfectly at home. For me that was extraordinary, I had never known it before. Was this due to Peter? Had he some special relationship with these people that made anyone he brought here a welcome guest? They seemed to radiate goodwill. It was this that gave the feeling of being flooded with warmth and benevolence.

But, at the bottom of it all was the strangest riddle: their language - or the lack of it. They really seemed, as far as I could see, never to use speech to communicate with one another. They didn't seem to need it. Yet there were never any signs of misunderstanding between them. They must communicate somehow. But how?

Was language necessary? We took it absolutely for granted. Life would be impossible without it - and yet, after all, it was a very cumbersome way to communicate. Speech led to endless misunderstandings and complications. An awful lot of talk was mere chatter, quite unnecessary. But when it came to anything positive! How could they ask a question, for instance, or pass a thought? Some people were supposed to be able to do it without words. Was it possible? Or did we just dismiss the idea because it seemed so highly improbable? Maybe, if I was open, I could 'catch' their thoughts. But how could you pass thoughts without language? Impossible! And yet these people must be doing it! Well, it was all too deep for me. Better forget it. I went down again to the lagoon.

Peter had lent me a mask and I lay face down, marvelling at this underwater world. The whole lagoon seemed to be alive with an endless pageant of colour and movement, an Aladdin's cave of living jewels! The fish! The tiny blue ones, chips of a midday sky; their friends in jade, the dandies, sunning themselves above the coral fans, proud of their crimson eyes; the goldfish with their violet spectacles; the black and sober square fish, aldermen, never in haste; the parrot fish, vicious, with bony beak, dressed in a peacock's tail; the pipe-fish, still as an old twig; the lemon man-in-the-street fish, drifting in crowds; fish ruled in straight lines or criss-crossed, like squared paper; blue fish barred with white and white fish barred with blue; fish busy feeding, idling away the day; frightened fish flashing for shelter; the rare and mottled balloon fish, swelling in fear; the deadly snake fish with its poisoned spines; the gaudy mullet coming out at night to paint the town red! There, anyway, was a whole world that managed very well without speech! I could have drifted on for hours just watching this endless parade of life beneath me; but the sun was too hot and at last I had to come out and take to the shade of the trees.

But as I turned to look out over the water, I was astonished to see quite a large motor cruiser coming in through the break in the reef a few hundred yards from where I was sitting. It turned and dropped anchor quite close to the beach.

This totally unexpected intrusion into 'my' island threw me right off balance. Somehow the idea of anyone else coming here, even knowing the island existed, had never crossed my mind. I didn't know what to do. I didn't want to meet these people, whoever they were. I didn't want to see them wandering about. I didn't want to acknowledge their existence. The whole thing irritated and angered me. If they started exploring, they would be bound to meet people. Would they get the same sort of welcome I'd got? I found myself getting very jealous, very possessive. I wanted to scare them off, drive them out, never see them again.

Meanwhile they had launched their dinghy. There were four of them, three men and a girl, they started up the outboard and made for the beach. They pulled their inflatable up on the sand and stood looking round. Three of them were just kids in their early twenties, the fourth, a man, looked nearer forty, probably the captain and the owner of the boat. He turned to walk along the beach in my direction and the others followed. I was already in the shade of the trees and now moved back so that I would not be seen. From the way they walked and looked about them, they did not seem to me to be just holiday makers putting in to the island to stretch their legs and have a dip in the lagoon. They kept stopping and looking round and as they got nearer I could hear some of their conversation.

'Funny, this dark sand.'

'Lava. The mountain must have erupted sometime.'

'Looks quiet now.'

'Good broad beach. You could put down here, Dino?'

'Sure. Plenty of room.'

The three men were in bathing trunks. The girl wore a white shirt, open, over her bra. There was a trace of foreign accent in the way they spoke.

44

'It's very beautiful here.' This from the girl.

'Wonder if there's fresh water.'

'The break in the reef's a bit narrow.'

'A couple of sticks of dynamite will fix that.' The older man laughed as he spoke, a dry laugh. His voice had an edge to it. His attitude seemed more incisive, more aggressive than the others.

'I wonder if the place is inhabited.'

'Probably not. It is not marked on the chart.'

They had stopped again, surveying the place, sizing it up. 'Might do us nicely. Off the regular track. About the right size. Good beach. What d'you think, Luiz?'

'I think we should explore. Tomas, you take Rita and see how it looks beyond the point. Go as far north as you can. I will go over the hill with Dino. See what we find. We all meet at the dinghy in one hour, yes?'

'Okay.'

The girl and Tomas evidently regarded this as an order and set off at a brisk pace back along the coast. Luiz, the older man who was obviously in charge of the operation they had come for, whatever it was, stood looking the place over, then he turned to Dino.

'I like this island, Dino. It is romantic. It has got something about it. Do you agree?'

'Yes. If there are natives for labour . . .'

'Well, perhaps it may have that also!'

The two men started to walk up the slope towards the isthmus, which I knew would soon bring them in sight of the estuary, the fish nets and obvious signs of the island being inhabited. I wondered how people would deal with these intruders. I decided to follow and see.

They soon came to one of the huts, exactly like the one belonging to Roka and Pili, and not far from it.

I heard Luiz saying to his companion. 'So, there are people here!' He was looking around at the hut with its thatched roof and the bags of things hanging up under the rafters. 'Primitive, but the work is not bad, eh, Dino?'

'Yes. I wonder where the people are.'

Luiz was examining the mats, the floor, the rough crocks and noticing the cleanliness and neatness everywhere.

'These people are not quite simple, not quite stone age. Curious. Maybe the Church has been here.'

The two walked on. I noticed, with some satisfaction, that there was nobody about. People had discreetly withdrawn, kept out of sight, but the two strangers had not noticed it.

But when they reached the brow of the low hill and looked over into the estuary, then their excitement and satisfaction were almost too much for them.

'Dino! Look at that!'

Dino just whistled.

'It's a natural, Dino! It's a natural!'

'With that island curling round! Make a perfect swimming pool!'

'With a jetty at the end to keep out the swells!'

'And the sharks!'

'Clear away those fish nets and the huts above on the slope there. Perfect for a restaurant, a snack bar.'

'And a disco!'

'And look at the terraces below here. Perfect for bungalows! We could get in huts for a hundred people, two hundred!'

'It's our dreamboat, Luiz. It's a natural!'

They went on in the same strain for some time. But I had heard enough. Now I knew exactly what these people were. They were just a gang of small-time tourist developers, looking for a likely site. If they found a place they fancied, all they had to do was to get a permit in Manila. With the Filipino economy the way it was, anything that would earn money, particularly tourism which spelt dollars, would never be refused. It meant they'd as good as bought the island. In six months the whole place would be ruined.

After more talk, they turned back towards the beach to tell the others about their find. I watched them go and went over to Roka's hut and sat on the edge of the floor, thinking.

I found I was seething with a kind of fury. It was typical of the world today. These people were ready to ruin anything in the name of development, walk into any place they fancied, trample on the locals, call in the bulldozers, pour the concrete and soon there would be the tawdry emptiness of a pleasure resort with all its 'amenities', its bars, its discos, its sex, self indulgence and greed. I determined there and then to do everything in my power to thwart these people. And the impulse got me to my feet to follow them, watch them, to see how I could do it.

They were coming down to the sea by the time I caught up with them. The other couple had returned from their walk northwards along the shore and, evidently from their gestures, they hadn't found anything much. But the ravings of Luiz and Dino spread to the others almost at once and nothing would satisfy them but that all four should return up the hill to see the estuary. I was too far away to hear what they said, but the sound of their excited voices echoed through the woods. However I noticed that not a single one of the inhabitants appeared. Somehow or other they knew or had been told to keep away.

The intruders remained at this pitch of energetic action all afternoon. They went back to the dinghy and put off to the boat, returning with sketch pads, cameras, glasses and so on. They went down through the terraces to the water's edge, walked along, examining the shore.

As I watched them it seemed to me they thought of themselves already as owners of the island and were busy planning and laying it out to meet the imperious needs of tourism.

It was quite late before they slackened off and decided to take a swim and begin to think about food. They made several trips back to the boat, brought over a sort of hamper and, when the boys had gathered sticks for a small fire, set about preparing an evening meal. They were all in high spirits and in no hurry to go back on board. Rita cleared away supper and the men were still finishing their wine before the sun went down and the moon rose.

It was not until then that an incident arose which entirely altered my opinion of these strange, wonderful people who lived on the island. To sit on the moonlit shore of a tropical lagoon is a pretty romantic experience and it even brought these intruders into quite a relaxed state. But when they heard music and saw people approaching with armfuls of flowers, this on top of everything else, well it was marvellous.

Four girls appeared carrying huge heavy garlands of flowers in their arms. It was they who were making the music, their voices so low and sweet it seemed little more than a murmur on the evening air. They were preceeded by an old man, different from any of the men I had seen here before. He was bearded and wore a sort of cloak that added dignity to an already quite impressive appearance. In his arms he carried a basket of fruit which he laid on the ground before Rita, giving her a broad smile and making a deep ceremonious bow.

I must say I had been watching all this with mixed feelings. This deputation could have no idea at all of the sort of people to whom they were giving such a welcome. I even made a move to protest, but immediately felt Roka's hand on my arm. He had appeared quietly behind me. He put a finger to his lips. Wait! it said.

None of the people I had met here ever spoke and I had quite made up my mind that they never did. Yet now this old man began to speak! And speak in the flowery and unctuous manner of a born orator and moreover in a language I had never heard and - judging from the expression on the faces of the visitors - a language which they had never heard either.

'*Sas chereto olous! Cherete! Then eine momon e efcharistisiss mas, ala timi mas na dechtoume toson diakekrimenous episkeptas is to micro mas nyssi . . .*' He went on for some time mouthing these strange words - if words they were, for we were too far away to hear anything distinctly. '*Ke tora*' he went on, '*ke sass, amorfi kyrie, ke sas exoche kirie synchoreste mas . . .*' This was evidently asking them to accept these poor gifts of flowers which his girls had brought because, as he said this, he waved them forward.

There could be no doubt about the impression made by these four beautiful young women. With their soft breasts, the flowers in their hair, the garlands round their necks, when they leaned forward offering the flowers - which were different from any I had seen before - it was a perfect end to the strangers' day and they were obviously quite overwhelmed by this show of hospitality. The girls placed the heavy wreaths round the necks of their guests and before they had finished making exclamations of delight at their wonderful perfume, had withdrawn, leaving the old man bowing and bowing, before he too withdrew.

But hardly had they left when a sudden change began to overcome the four wretches seated on the ground. They lost all their gaiety. They began to yawn; they lay back and within half a minute they were all fast asleep.

I began to see how well all this charade on the beach had been thought out. No sooner had the visitors succumbed to the general anaesthetic contained in the flowers, than eight men, who had obviously been waiting, came down quickly onto the beach and picked up the drugged intruders. One taking the head and the other the feet, they carried them to the inflatable and laid them side by side in the bottom of it.

When all this was done the old man who had made the speech and another elderly assistant, went up to the side of the boat and remained standing there, looking down at the drugged figures with an intense expression in their eyes. All the others stood waiting till this ritual or ceremony or whatever it was, was over. Then as the old men signalled them to go ahead, they launched the boat and, one taking the line and the others pushing behind and at the sides, they all swam out to the cruiser.

Here one went up the companion way onto the deck and taking the line from the dinghy, made it fast to a cleat at the companion-way. Then he plunged back into the sea and the whole company swam ashore. The two elders waited to see all this completed and then, making a sign to the men, disappeared into the trees.

This little episode entirely changed my feelings about the island. These apparently 'simple' people had a sophisticated knowledge of anaesthetics. What was this drug that worked so smoothly and so quickly? Was it the natural scent of the flowers or was it added? How long did it last? Were there after effects? Could it be strengthened and made fatal? The whole thing amazed me and teemed with questions.

It was not until later when I had the chance to ask Peter about it that I learned how widespread and common, in this part of the world - especially among primitive tribes - was the knowledge of these natural drugs. They varied from the instantaneously fatal curari to a whole range of sleeping pills and sedatives. Their effectiveness I had seen for myself.

I think there may have been many who, like me, wanted to see how this affair ended, for occasionally I heard slight movements in the shadows nearby. Roka came up to me again and together we sat to wait for the dawn. We took it in turns to doze for it was quite a long wait. But there was no sign of any life or movement from the dinghy till the sun was up.

Then we saw Luiz sit up and, still half asleep, pull himself up the steps onto the deck. He hardly looked ashore, preoccupied with waking up the others still asleep in the boat below. He threw a bucket of sea water over them, but even this did not cause much reaction, but at last all of them, still looking heavily drugged, managed to throw their flowers into the sea and clamber on deck. Luiz shouted some orders, started the engines, got up the anchor and then, without a backward look at the island, the cruiser made her way through the break in the reef and stood out for deep water.

CHAPTER SIX

All the men who had been concerned with getting our visitors away now came out of hiding onto the shore and watched the boat disappearing in the distance. Then, with the wave of a hand to us, they moved off. Roka and I walked back across the isthmus in the glorious morning. I was feeling quite sleepy after our long vigil. When we reached his house, Roka saw me yawning, laughed, clapped me on the back and pointed to the mats. But Sibu and Riri had also seen us arrive and ran up, greeting me most affectionately.

Ever since I'd arrived on the island, I'd had this sense of welcome; it was in the air. Hospitality was as natural to these people as breathing; it was almost impersonal, a social gesture. But now there was quite a different feeling. It was warm and close. I felt part of the family. The girls knew I was leaving and would be sad to see me go.

But their way of showing me their feelings was unexpected. They set about giving me a general massage! It was a real workout. Useless to protest I wanted to sleep. They knew what was good for me and, as I soon found out, were experts at the job. Once I had submitted I found I began to enjoy it. Riri took over my feet and my legs, working on the soles and toe joints, while Sibu attacked the tensions in my neck and shoulders, pressing and kneading, then working over my chest and stomach, rolling me over to loosen up my spine, vertebra by vertebra. It was all done with such vigour and goodwill that within twenty minutes I felt a new man and was even ready to engage Sibu in other forms of massage. But this was laughingly refused. Now I needed to sleep and, as if to show they meant it, Sibu put a pillow under my head and the two girls abruptly withdrew.

Peter must have come in so low over the water I hardly heard his approach till the aircraft rolled to rest at almost the same place where we first landed - was it possible? - only two days earlier! When I got down to the beach I saw him already standing with about half a dozen island men. From the way they stood and their inward looking expressions, I assumed they were, in the island's way, 'discussing' something. It was Peter who broke off to greet me warmly.

'John! Had a good weekend?'

I grasped his outstretched hand and pumped it extra-vagantly, unable to speak. And that wordless greeting was somehow witness to all the island had already taught me - that when it came to anything important, words were perfectly useless.

Quite a lot of people seemed to have collected, evidently knowing in their own mysterious way that Peter would arrive. They seemed to hold him in some especial esteem and, by his bearing before them, I too began to see him in a different light. I threw my pack into the backseat of the cabin; but when the crowd that had collected saw that Peter was immediately leaving them again, they burst into song. Strange how deeply it stirred me. I found it almost unbearably poignant. They seemed to pluck a moment of sadness out of time and offer it up, like a prayer, for the safety and peace of those they loved.

We stood still, listening till it was over, and then climbed aboard. Peter started the engines, opened up and took off. We shot away over the water. Suddenly it was all gone. Over. We had left that world, as if it had never been. We were back in the terrors of the world we knew.

I can't remember anything about the flight. I saw nothing. I found I didn't want to talk. And I saw Peter didn't either. One of his engines was running rough. He was evidently bothered about this, calling Control, getting priority to land and so on. We taxied to the place reserved for private planes, where he gave some orders to a mechanic. His car was nearby and it was only then that he spoke:

'Look. I know you want to talk. So do I. But I've got a busy day. Rosa's going down to see her family - they live on Mindanao - and I have to see her off at the airport. I've got meetings all afternoon and a banquet tonight, which means that I shan't be free till about nine. Come up to my flat then - it's on the top floor. Okay?'

'Well, at last!' he greeted me, as he let me in. 'I thought I'd never get free! Whisky?' He poured drinks for us both, adding soda and ice and talking as he did so. 'I expect you're bursting with questions! I hope you'll forgive me for pretending I was putting you down on a desert island; but I had my reasons. I'll explain all that later. But tell me, how did it strike you - the feel of the place, I mean?'

I said, 'Peter, I've been so loaded with new impressions, new emotions, I really haven't sorted it out yet. I suppose you might say that somehow it's changed my life - if you see what I mean. I feel a different man. I really don't know how I'm going to cope with all the old emptiness, I really don't.'

Peter was listening very intently.

'You see I had absolutely no idea what sort of a weekend I was in for, but no sooner had you left and I was alone there, than I began to feel that strange atmosphere the place has. So still, so rich! It was something I had never known before and then as things began to happen, they were all so new, so utterly unexpected -

54

Sibu actually rode a dolphin that turned up in the lagoon on my first evening. Amazing! And the way they hummed while I was eating supper with them and then the way we all slept together . . . It was all so easy, so different. It made me see what terribly narrow lives we lead, how other, wonderful ways to live are possible. Of course we see all this sort of thing on TV and take it quite for granted; but when you really get into the experience, it's utterly different.'

I stopped then. It wasn't only this that had meant so much to me. 'But you see, Peter,' I went on, 'it's much more than that. It raises all those questions we were talking about before I left. It's really all that which has turned everything upside down for me.'

Peter looked across at me with great warmth. 'I'm delighted, John! I really am! I had a hunch it might pay off. Something told me this was for you. But you do realize, don't you, that it has to be kept secret? The island is, literally, out of this world. The more you share their lives, the more you realize it has a sort of simplicity about it that's near perfection. We're all so resigned to the idea that perfection belongs to the future, it's difficult to believe it when you suddenly see it right under your nose! Here! Now!'

Peter paused for a moment and shook his head. 'But the question is: how long can it last . . .?'

'You heard about those people in the cruiser?'

Peter laughed. 'Oh, yes! That sort of thing has happened before, you know. They're quite up to seeing such people off. No problem!'

'The whole thing was pretty impressive, Peter. I must say it shook me. When I first noticed they didn't speak, I couldn't make it out, but gradually I began to accept that they really had no language, didn't know how to speak. So when I heard all those words pouring out of that old man, I simply couldn't believe it.'

'It was Greek actually. Theo loves playing jokes.'

'Theo?'

'Yes. The old man you heard talking was Theo. He is the heart of the whole extraordinary business. I met him absolutely by chance. It really was the strangest coincidence - if you can call it that. I'd only been out here about a year when one morning a doctor at the hospital, a man I'd happened to meet at a dinner party, rang me up and asked me if I spoke Greek. I suppose I must have mentioned that my mother was Greek and he'd remembered it. Anyhow he said they had a chap in from one of the islands, he didn't know which, who said he was Greek. Nobody could make sense talking to him - he spoke practically no English - so could I come along and translate? It would be a great help. So of course I went along and that was how I met Theo.'

Peter paused, evidently full of memory.

'He had some outlandish Greek name - Parapanopoulos or something - but everyone called him Theo. It suited him somehow. I shall never forget the first time I set eyes on him. He really was the most extraordinary looking chap. Lying there in the bed, terribly thin, with his pale hollow cheeks, wispy beard, half bald ... but what you couldn't forget, what made his face memorable, so that I still see it today as plainly as I saw it then, were his eyes! In that scraggy, careworn face, they were dancing! Dancing John - and I mean dancing. I have never seen eyes so full of life, so vivid, so absolutely free from care, pain, anxiety, from anything related to his own condition. He was the happiest man I had ever seen in my life - and it affected everyone, doctors, nurses, visitors, cleaners, the ambulance men who brought him in, they all kept on stopping by, just to see how he was getting on, any excuse to visit, to be near him really. Something came from him, John. I don't know how to say it without sounding sententious, but it was something ... purity, holiness ... He was more alive than anyone I have ever met in my life - ever shall meet probably.'

'Was he dying?'

'Doomed, so the doctors told me. Inoperable cancer. Just a question of how long he would last. But of course he didn't know that, or pretended he didn't, just mentioned in passing that he was in for a few days, some trouble with a bit of constipation, nothing much.

'And talk! Nothing could stop him - and as I was the only one who could understand him, he poured it all out to me. The nurses and doctors tried to tell him he must rest, must relax and all that; but as soon as I appeared he was off. Life story right through from his teenage days when he got himself ordained and admitted to Mount Athos. Ten years there. "My knees have never really recovered from the genuflections!" he said. But then he decided that there was nothing more to be found there. He'd learned all they could teach him and it wasn't enough. The world was changing and they were still stuck in the old rituals, "No good, no good." he kept on repeating. So he left. Great scandal of course. The family. His mother weeping herself to sleep. His father calling him a heretic ... But of course there were big gaps. How did he get himself to America? As a sailor probably. But he didn't say. And Panama? He probably worked his passage there and on to the New Hebrides. Then another gap. How did he get hold of that boat? How he talked about that boat! I suppose he loved it more than anything in life. It was his passport to freedom, to the unknown, to something - he didn't know what - that would be the crown and blessing of his life.'

'What sort of a boat?'

'She was called the *Aphrodite*, an old wooden five-tonner, probably built at the turn of the century. Good solid oak timbers, probably a very good sea boat, double ender, but of course a bit leaky by now - and you know what the Greeks are, good sailors, but not so hot at looking after things. Anyhow he seems to have had a lot of fun, going from island to island, working his way across and up through the Coral Sea and the Moluccas northwards towards Manila. On his way to where? I never could understand and I don't think he could either. It was just predestination and it came in the form of a typhoon which drove poor little *Aphrodite* onto the reef at the island, smashed her to bits and threw him up, half drowned into the lagoon . . .'

Peter paused. 'Care for the other half?' He got up and refilled our glasses. When he sat down again there was a sort of wonder in his eyes.

'Isn't it extraordinary? This little renegade Pappas from Mount Athos, wandering half across the world, as if drawn by some remorseless destiny to end up in perhaps the only place where his own absolutely original view of life could be used. What about the "destiny that shapes our ends, rough hew them though we may"? Anyway of course they took him in, patched him up - he'd got a broken leg and bad bruises - apart from being nearly drowned - and in a few days, just as it had been in hospital, everyone was at his feet! It was something about him. He inspired devotion, love, tenderness. Everybody wanted to look after him, serve him, fuss him. And he took nothing! It was wonderful, wonderful, John! I remember him saying, "They had nothing to give but love! Nothing! A bit of cloth to cover me, a fan, a flower for what little hair I have left - and that was all - but it was more than enough. Dear God, I would have crossed ten worlds, braved a hundred typhoons to serve such love . . .!

'But now comes the tricky bit, the bit that people can't take, can't believe, the fact he soon found out, that the people on his island didn't speak, had no language and communicated somehow by a mixture of instinct, telepathy and observation which served them very well. Far better, Theo said, than all the chatter we use to mess up our lives. Of course there's plenty of evidence of this sort of thing, if we look for it - I mean catching other people's thoughts, knowing what they are thinking, feeling, without translating it - usually very badly, very incompletely - into speech. We all do it a bit without thinking about it. Sometimes when we find we have passed a thought to our neighbour, we just laugh and call it "telepathy" - and when we have labelled it, forget all about it . . . But we all have it, more or less, and if we took it seriously, thought about it, cultivated it, I am quite sure these talents, powers or whatever you like to call them could be developed. Those people on the island have done it, after all. It's in their genes now. It's in them when they are born . . .' Peter paused again.

'I shall never forget his face, John, sitting in that chair you're sitting in now . . .'

'Sitting here!' I couldn't resist interjecting. 'Did they operate? Did they save him? Did he go back to the island?'

'They operated, did what they could. It would give him a few weeks respite, a couple of months perhaps. But they did not want him dying in the hospital. So they told him he was okay, pretty well convalescent really, and it wasn't necessary for him to stay in hospital any longer. So he came here. It was perfect for him really and I was glad to be able to offer it to him. No steps to climb, air-conditioning, a comfortable bed and one of the girls from the hospital coming in every day just to see if he wanted anything. He just lay there and talked. But what I most remember were his eyes! Those marvellous big wide open eyes that danced with excitement, with joy, with love, that made you feel he couldn't die, that he would, could, must live for ever . . .'

Peter looked across at me and I could see from the way he leaned forward and spoke, the effect that Theo had had on him. He was quite carried away with it all. 'I remember the day he told me that "his" people on the island had no language, didn't speak. He was quite overcome with the wonder of it. "I fell on my knees and gave thanks to God!" he said. "Don't you see, Peter! Speech is the damnation of the human race!" And he rushed on in a torrent of words, "I always felt we talked too much, argued too much, quarrelled too much - but how could we help it? That was life! And now, here were these people, somehow or other, by some miraculous quirk of destiny, born in such a way their brains had never developed, couldn't develop, speech - and so made free to become what humanity should be: the crown of the creation! Talking has severed us from all the latent powers we are capable of developing, powers we have disregarded, thrown away, scoffed at as being ridiculous mystical nonsense - when actually they are the key to all development - and imprisoned us in words, our everlasting source of misunderstanding and division. Words! Even at their best, for anything important, we know quite well they are no good at all!"'

Peter paused, obviously deeply stirred by the story he had told. Then he went on. 'Of course, John, you understand, I didn't really believe him. I took him and his island with a pinch of salt. I knew there were said to be primitive tribes, still in the Stone Age, living on some of the islands; but this was something else. So when he suddenly said a couple of weeks later that now he was feeling fine and really couldn't idle about any longer, I was surprised. And then when he asked me, as a last favour, if I would take him back, I was astonished.

'"Take you back?" I said. "Where?"

'"To the island. Where else?"

'"But how?" I really couldn't spare the time for a sea trip.

'"In that little plane you're so proud of. Would it be too much trouble? It isn't so far . . ."

'"And where do we land?" I was just humouring him. It was such an outlandish idea.

'"There's quite a good long beach, firm sand too."

'I just stared at him. "Have you got a map?" I said.

'"No I'm afraid not. But I can take you there."

'"But Theo, I can't just take off into the blue. I've got to tell the Tower my destination, probable time of arrival and so on."

'"Oh, don't worry about that. Give them the name of any island roughly on the same compass course, say 190 magnetic, and leave the rest to me." I was surprised when he gave me a bearing, but after all he was a seaman. "We have to keep quiet about the place, Peter. The last thing we want are tourists. But if you fly at sea level, keep under their radar, we'll be quite okay."

'I really couldn't argue. He had the same power over me he had over everyone else. But the practical way he'd thought the whole thing out, taken it for granted I'd do what he wanted, was endearing - and after all he was a sick man. The most important thing was to get him back to that island of his. I just wanted to please him and, if what the doctors had said was true, he mightn't have long to go. So, against my better judgement, I agreed. We got him down to the car. He was weaker than I'd realized and needed help. At the airport it was quite a struggle to get him into the plane; but finally we made it and I took off.

'It was a strange sort of situation. Here I was, with a man I hardly knew - except that he was very sick - taking off into the blue in an absolutely nonchalant way, without a map, at sea level, to an island that wasn't marked on the charts! But he was enjoying every moment of it. "Nothing like flying is there?" he observed with a smile that seemed to take in the whole sky. "Pity I never learned to fly ... Keep to the right a bit, Peter, just a bit ... that's it ..." Then he went off to sleep and I made a note of the bearing. I might have to make the journey again on my own. After about an hour - at sea level, don't forget - he woke up.

'"I've been in touch. They're expecting us. They'll be there." I smiled at him. Crackers!

'"How long now?" I asked.

'"About an hour. The mountain'll be coming up over the horizon any minute now." And, of course, it did. There was the long wide beach, just as he'd said. And as we came closer, the crowd of people he promised on the sand. I'd never seen the island before, but as there are about 7000 of them about, that wasn't suprising. Anyhow I circled to check on my approach and put down. As soon as I had switched off, the crowd ran down to surround us. I suppose they had never seen an aircraft close to before. But when they saw that Theo was with me! Then their surprise and exultation was overwhelming. They burst into such a chorus of joy that it left me sitting there with my mouth open! You see I had never heard them sing before and their welcome was of such sheer beauty and wonder it fairly took my breath away. It was marvellous, John, marvellous ...'

At that moment the phone rang. Peter took up the receiver and, after a moment, handed it over. 'London on the line for you,' he said. It was my boss, telling me that the Sydney conference had been changed again and could I get down there on the next plane? I said I would do what I could and phone him on arrival.

My irritation at having Peter's story broken so abruptly gave way almost at once to all the queries and practical arrangements that had to be made to get me away next day and somehow or other the chance for him to finish his story never came back. But I had become so fascinated by what he had told me I didn't want to leave that part of the world without hearing more, much more, about Theo and the island. I suppose the truth was my weekend there had got me so hooked on the place that I simply had to come back. So I asked Peter if he could put up with my returning for a few days on my way through to London. His reply was immediate.

'Please do. I've got a lot more to tell you - and things to discuss with you too.'

At the airport he enlarged on it all a bit. 'As a matter of fact, Theo and the Elders seem to be in a bit of a tizzy about things. Premonition and all that. They've got a sort of tame oracle who keeps prophesying all sorts of disasters. Nonsense probably, but if anything did blow up, I'd like to have you around.'

My flight was called. 'Well thanks a lot for everything.' I took his hand. 'More than words can say!'

We both laughed at our very private joke.

CHAPTER SEVEN

It took about an hour for the flight to settle down. I put on a pair of slippers, tipped my seat back and tried to doze. But I found I was too wound up to sleep. Vivid pictures of all I had seen and felt poured through my head in a torrent. I could go over the hours almost minute by minute, from the moment when we had swooped down to the island and all those memories, run together, made a sunlit haze of happiness, a picture of a never-never land which couldn't possibly exist - and yet did exist! I had seen it, touched it, felt it. I could come back to it!

Could I? Or would something intervene? Somehow prevent me from returning? The mere thought of it filled me with alarm. I felt how suddenly, deeply, I had been touched by it all. By what? It was something more than mere excitement, novelty at a new experience, something more than ease, happiness, something more than those silences which bred such peace. Imposed silence, after all had been a common monastic rule for centuries. But the islanders' silences were quite different. They were living silences, nature's silences, the silences of a summer morning when the life of all living creatures is carried on the communion of the wind, shared, understood and complete.

Suddenly I saw something I had never seen before. Words were the enemy of truth! It was difficult for feelings to lie, for looks to lie, for acts to lie; but words, our great hypocrisy, poured out, endlessly hiding the truth. Speech, vaunted as the noble vehicle of learning, of poetry, philosophy and literature, was, at the same time, a shocking gusher of lies, creating the endless muddling and befuddling of all humanity.

The rest of the creation hid nothing. With its loves and hates, habits, needs and fears, all nature lived openly in truth. Yet our superior humanity endlessly patronized her, meddled with her, plundered her for gain or greed. A creature that could not speak was obviously inferior. Yet the proud speaking world was growing mortally sick, crushed under the remorseless weight of too much of it.

Love, hate, grief and pity were beyond words. Were there other ways to communicate, deeper subtler powers by which to learn, to understand? Was it this those grotesque figures were telling me? - to learn through the senses, not through speech which had almost entirely usurped the place of all sensual experience.

But one thing I knew for certain: I was determined to get back, longed to get back, not to research the life of a 'primitive' tribe - far more civilized than we were - but simply because I wanted to learn from them how to live in simplicity and truth. Or was it just because I had begun to love them?

The Australian conference kept me pretty busy, the discussions were lively and the general increase in awareness of the need to improve soils, stimulate research into better crops, keep abreast of the growing resistance of pests and, in general to improve farming efficiency throughout the whole South Pacific area meant, as far as we were concerned, many enquiries for our products and a full order book to take back to the UK.

I ought, of course, to have been pleased about this. And I was. It was good for the firm, and good for me personally. But I found that while I was keeping up appearances, making the right answers, doing all the things I had been doing for twenty years, it was all quite empty. I didn't believe in it any more.

I had told Peter I wasn't happy about the way my life was going, that I felt it was leading me nowhere; but now! It had suddenly become quite intolerable. All the time at the back of my mind was the thought of getting back to the island. How could a couple of days on a tropical island in the company of simple people, with apparently nothing particularly special about them, completely change one's life? It was impossible, ridiculous. Yet there it was.

And, at the same time, I really couldn't say what it was that drew me . . . it kept me awake at nights. When I tried to analyse it, what place could I possibly have in that life? Did I want to throw everything over and live there like a savage? I should be bored stiff in a week. What could I do? I couldn't help them, serve them. In many ways I needed help more that they did. It was my life that was in a mess, not theirs!

So the thing went round and round in my head and I was glad I was returning via Manila. I needed to talk to Peter and try to see the whole thing more clearly. Time and time again my thoughts came back to language - or rather the lack of it. It was this that set the place apart from anything I had ever known. The more you thought about it the more baffling it became. Not to speak cut out huge areas of daily life. Could there even be thought without language? Certainly I'd had thoughts which I couldn't put into words; but was this because they were not thoughts but feelings? Where did thought end and feeling begin? Could there be thoughts not translated into speech? If people did not speak or write, could they think at all? And what went on inside to fill those silences, those marvellous silences when all problems seemed to be dissolved? It was a riddle.

The whole question of communication became fascinating. I was convinced these people could communicate, but it certainly wasn't through speech. Then how did they do it? The idea of thought transference makes us all feel slightly uncomfortable. It smells of mediums and mystical hankypanky. But is it so mysterious? Maybe it is happening all the time! How often do we have that curious feeling in conversation that the other person had caught our thinking, and we don't need to translate it into speech? We don't pay much attention to this, just laugh about it and call it telepathy - but could it be developed? Is it, so to speak, dormant within us, lost over the centuries through lack of use?

Occasionally we get glimpses, usually from the stories of travellers who have happened to come close to the lives of primitive tribes, that they have mysterious ways of knowing what is happening, or is about to happen, and this is as normal to them as speech is to us. We have read about witch doctors who were rainmakers or could 'call' animals or fish, who knew the future and could tell you what was going to happen; why should it surprise us to find a community still using such powers? They, naturally, would find our cacophony of speech incredibly funny and clumsy, like the jabbering of baboons. You can pass a thought instantaneously. Talk round it for an hour and you can still get it wrong! Better to keep the human voice for singing, to express joy and give thanks to God. That was how they used it on the island.

Maybe the island was more than an escape to paradise. Maybe this chance freak, no more than a fortunate mutation of genes, could lead us to a totally new conception of the way to live. Nobody would see it, of course, until our present so-called civilization broke down. But maybe the future would view this maniac faith in speech and the materialism that grew from it as a huge, disgusting boil which had to be lanced before our long-suffering planet could develop normally. Maybe life on the island existed just to show us that?

CHAPTER EIGHT

'There's one thing I wanted to ask you about Theo.'

I was back in Manila, sitting with Peter in his flat after supper.

'Isn't it a sort of miracle, Peter? After all, you told me he was doomed, couldn't possibly live and yet here he is, now, still pretty convincingly alive it seemed to me.'

'Yes, it is a miracle. He always says it's the island and the people. They cured him, he says. It may be true. Or perhaps the medics in Manila were wrong, that he wasn't as ill as they thought, or maybe their operation was more successful than they knew. Anyhow, there he is. Still going strong!'

'How long ago was all this, Peter?'

'I took him back to the island exactly nine years ago,' Peter replied, 'and, as far as I can make out, he was on the island altogether for about nine years before that, but it may have been a bit more or less. Nine was a sacred number to him.'

'So he's been on the island for almost twenty years. They obviously worship him, but they'd been there, presumably, for centuries before he came, living a decent, simple life. What has he really done for them, Peter? Has he changed their laws, altered their customs, taught them Christianity, or what?'

'I didn't really find out much about that until I took to visiting the island fairly regularly. Then it gradually began to dawn on me that there was practically nothing he hadn't helped them with, but he did it all so lightly, so carefully, it always seemed they had done it themselves. Almost at once, he told me, he saw they were a quite unique people and that he had dropped into a unique situation. It was a sort of Golden Age, a golden opportunity, a clean slate. Just imagine! A people with no money, no property that wasn't shared, nothing written down - and so no laws, no precedents, no heirarchies, but way above that, no language, no speech, and so none of the hell we have created for ourselves with our dreadful imaginations, our everlasting quarrels which can only end up in the madness and waste of wars.'

'Yes, of course. If there was no money, no property, no laws, there'd be no sense in all the paraphernalia we've set up. There'd be no motive for it!'

'Yes. That's the key! No motive! I remember his enthusiasm, his excitement, at realizing that. At first, he told me that like you - and me, too - he felt lost because he couldn't communicate with anybody except by signs. But very soon the whole question became a terrific challenge to him. What had happened? What strange genetic quirk had changed the basic balance of their whole psyche? You see, we are all head-orientated. We refer everything to our heads. Our feelings are something we take for granted and, on the whole, we find them rather a nuisance, getting in the way of what we think. But these people have reversed all that, they refer everything to their feelings, so they haven't "developed", as we say, by dreaming up madness in their heads. So they're very simple, very direct, very sane.'

'It's all fascinating, Peter, absolutely fascinating. My old Dad used to say a man's feelings are his values, what he is, and that leads him straight to morality, conscience.'

Peter nodded. 'Yes. It's having a clear conscience that gives these people their wonderful state. They're so relaxed, they've nothing to hide.'

'Even their lovemaking!'

'Yes, even that; and even that in a way is due to Theo. Actually I think his most important contribution to the whole life of the island may be the fact that he found a way to control their birthrate.'

'The birthrate!'

'Yes, it was his most important problem. I suppose in the beginning the idea of limiting population was never even thought of; but as it increased, they began to see there wasn't enough food to go round. Babies were undernourished and some people would soon be facing starvation. So the Elders held a long consultation and finally came to what was really a terrible decision - to destroy the mouths they could not feed.'

'Kill the children!'

'Yes; but, you know, curiously enough there's a record that the ancient Tahitians, in the days before Bougainville and Cook turned up, had the same problem and came to the same decision. What authority their chiefs must have had to make such a decree and have it carried out!'

'Dreadful! But weren't there even primitive means of abortion?'

'It appears not.'

'But it's mindless, stupid. They could have economized, grown more food -'

'Apparently the idea of crops never occurred to them. Like all really primitive people, they just lived off what the land, the forests, the lakes or seas provided. I believe the idea of cultivation, cropping, comes quite a lot later in human development. Anyhow here nobody had thought of it, evidently.'

'But the women! Didn't the women protest, go on strike or something!'

'Yes, here they certainly did. That was the situation Theo found when he arrived. He told me how he saw a two day old infant having its skull crushed with a stone.'

'Ghastly!'

'He shouted at them, cursed them. Of course it made no difference. They had no speech. Nobody understood him. It was then he first made his vow to learn their way of communication. And then came his moment of inspiration. He knew about, or found (I never quite understood which) a root that grew here. He told them if they chewed a bit of it every morning, they'd have no more babies! When they tried it and found it really worked, well, you can imagine!'

'Must have practically sterilized the island!'

'Practically. But then Theo added another inspired idea. He told them that to bear a child was an honour. Marriage was a sacrament. As the population couldn't be allowed to grow to much more than a thousand, it would be necessary to limit the yearly births to nine. This would about balance the rate at which people were dying off.'

'Extraordinary!'

'Yes. It set up a new morality for the whole place and solved the impossible problem of sex. Simple people living a fairly easy life have healthy sexual appetites. Why not let them get on with it? All our religious or moral principles meant nothing to them. Theo put it on a quite prosaic level. Men and women, he said, manufacture sex material in their bodies which, every so often, has to be got rid of. Sex is really a cleansing process. It was as simple as that! No religion. No morality. No sin. Just plain commonsense. It wasn't very romantic; but it was exceedingly practical!'

'But isn't there something more than that here, Peter? I mean I don't get any impression of immorality, depravity. On the contrary I feel a pure, almost spiritual quality in everything.'

'Of course, this island has a caring society, a deeply

moral society; but sex plays a big part in it and you have to give sex its place. Anyhow, Theo gave it quite a different look by announcing what he called the Festival of the First Spring Days. This is a yearly jamboree, a sort of safety valve for their high spirits. Special liquor is brewed for this one night only. Well, it certainly loosens people up! And what with the feasting, the dancing and the general hilarity, it ends in a free-for-all in which everybody, as far as I can make out, has romps with everyone else. You need quite a lot of stamina to last it out, believe me!'

'I'd like to be invited!'

'Why not? You'd be welcome. But you see how wonderfully intuitive and sensitive Theo was? He encouraged sex by taking off all the brakes and at the same time limited it by concentrating it round a festival, so it never got out of hand. Then, by insisting in the sacredness of birth, he cleansed it all. Lovemaking is one thing, a new human being quite another. So, as there are only to be nine births a year, you can imagine the competition to be one of the mothers or husbands.'

'Doesn't it lead to free fights?'

'No. Actually, it's amazingly good tempered. The old men choose youths for their courage, strength or skill. The women girls for their beauty and I suppose what you would call their "womanliness", and then about a couple of weeks before the marriage day, the island gets together to choose. That usually takes some time. But when it's decided, the island holds its most beautiful festival of the year, usually in May, which ends with a wonderful torchlight procession to that dell you saw. Each couple is given a pavilion. With much ceremony the hanging walls are let down and the whole community joins in that marvellous singing to bless their union . . .

'Like no other singing I've ever heard.'

'Yes. And there the couples live together till their babies are born, all more or less at the same time, which leads to another celebration and that leads on to a third when the babies are weaned and given away . . .'

'Given away? Who to? Why?'

'Because - and this again showed Theo's own special sensitivity of instinct - he knew from his own Greek childhood how all parents ruin their children by spoiling them, letting them get their own way and so fostering all sorts of selfishness and egoism which will ruin their chances of becoming good members of the community. And especially a community on an island like this, which depends for its success on the way everybody lives for everybody else. So, as they all love children, foster parents are the rule and - well, you've seen the results. People do not belong to each other, set up family feuds and all that. Parents can be with their children of course, but they can't live under the same roof.'

'And how do they choose the foster parents?'

'There's no rule, as far as I can see. Probably someone the mother likes - take Roka and Pili. Sibu is no relation to them, nor Riri. It's just worked out like that. Some couples have no young people with them, some have five or six. It doesn't matter.'

'There's no marriage, then?'

'No. None. Just as there's no property. Nobody belongs to anybody else. Of course some couples do "fall in love" and stay together all their lives. Why not? But usually there's a bit of moving around till middle age when they settle down for good.'

'But it can't all be sweetness and light, Peter. There must be disagreements, rows, fights. What happens then?'

'There are surprisingly few. All crime is treated in the same way. The wrong doer is tied up, head and foot to a tree. And the tree is usually near some welltrodden path. So everybody sees him, knows what he's done and can spit at him, hit him - but not too much or they get the same treatment themselves! He's left there, in the heat of the sun, without food or water, till he "repents". Usually one day is enough. If it's more serious the prisoner has to remain there for two, three or four days, but that's rare. But they've got a lot of humour about punishment, too. If a woman behaves badly, if she's bossy, rough or cheats her neighbours, the others just get together, hold her down and paint half her face white. It takes a few days to wear off, so everyone knows and makes jokes about her. It's the same with the men, only they get half their hair shaved off. It's the stocks, the old pillory really.'

'That's wonderful, Peter. Far better for people to feel shame at what they've done than just to shut them away and then let them out as if nothing had happened. But what about serious crime? Murder for instance?'

'I only remember one case. The man was sick, very violent, impossible to control and finally killed the woman he was living with. He was hit over the head from behind. There was no trial. Everybody knew what he had done. He didn't feel it. It was as quick and humane as possible.'

'Pity, all the same.'

'Yes. But what can you do? This is a pragmatic community. There's no prison. You can't shut a man up. If you keep him alive it will need at least two other men to look after him. That's unacceptable. So there it is.'

'And death?'

'There's no dead on the island. Everybody is buried at sea, the day they die.'

'All these things work in a small community. I don't know if they'd work if it were bigger.'

'Maybe they shouldn't be bigger. Maybe that's one of the places where we've gone wrong.'

'Maybe. You know, Peter, what I got from my weekend? What I carried away and bring back now, is an overall feeling of warmth and love - except from Sibu!'

'Why not from Sibu?'

'Well, she scared me. Her idea of love was to wrestle me to the ground and then sit on top of me!'

Peter burst out laughing. 'No! Did she really? She's quite a girl! How did you get into that?'

'Well, we'd all eaten those shells from the reef, you know ... I didn't realize they were aphrodisiacs. But suddenly there were Pili and Roka well away, and I saw what was expected of me. I couldn't face it, Peter, the way I've been brought up, and being, well, shy really, I suppose, I just bolted for the beach! But she outran me, grabbed me and pinned me down. I didn't know what was going to happen. But then she looked so marvellous, gave me such a feeling of desire and longing, it ... freed me somehow. It's something that never happened to me before. It ... well, it made me let go. I've never known anything like it ...

Peter couldn't get over it. He went on laughing for a long time. 'She must have wanted to show you what real love was! I don't suppose any man has ever refused her before! No wonder she went for you! And now I expect you've got your tongue hanging out and are just longing to get back?'

'I should be glad to see her, I admit.'

'Well, you're in luck. I've just had another of these curious signals, or messages, or whatever you like to call them. They want me to go down to the island and look them up. How long have you got?'

'A few days. I could stretch it to a week, maybe.'

'Then let's leave tomorrow - if I can square it with

Rosa, that is. By the way, not a word about the island.'

Rosa came into the room at that moment and went straight to her husband and kissed him. Peter had told me she was a beautiful girl and she certainly was. Slim and finely drawn, I sensed something Arabian in her femininity. When she gave me her hand, it felt as if I was shaking hands with fine porcelain. And her eyes, when she looked up at me, were warm and melting.

'So you are the friend of my Peter?' she smiled. I said I hoped I was and that we had known each other since college days.

'Promise not to take him away from me!'

It was a strange remark, made so suddenly; I was quite taken aback. Did she so desperately fear to lose him? Why? She was evidently young and deeply in love.

'I have no intention of taking him away from you.' I laughed. 'I can't imagine anyone wanting to leave you,' I added. She deserved the compliment.

'No? But my Peter is so strange.' She kissed Peter again. 'Why are you so strange, darling?'

Peter laughed lightly and turned to me. 'She thinks I have nothing to do but take care of her! Now,' and he put an arm round her, 'let's give Peter some lunch.'

The question of our trip was never mentioned, but Peter must have had his own way of fixing things. Anyway we left next morning early, before Rosa was up.

CHAPTER NINE

'One of the reasons I'm glad to have you back,' said Peter as we drove to the airport, 'is that I've been thinking. It's only an idea, but why don't you consider coming out this way - permanently, I mean. I feel you're more than just "interested" in the island. You feel for it and what it stands for more than I do. Maybe you have a part in its future, who knows? I'm not engaged in that way and, to tell you the truth, it's getting a bit much for me. I wanted to help Theo; but he seems all right now. He doesn't need me. But he needs someone, a sort of a link with the world.'

'It had crossed my mind, Peter. But it's a big decision. I'd have to go home first, anyway.'

'Of course. It's just my selfishness, really. But I don't like having secrets from Rosa and I'm so busy I can't get down there as often as I'd like to - and they do seem to be a bit jumpy about something . . .'

'About what, I wonder?'

'That's the trouble; I don't quite know. Theo always has these fears of "invasion", as he calls it, and I believe the Elders have premonitions of disasters. Probably all nonsense; but these days . . .'

'How d'you get these messages, Peter?' It was a question I'd long been wanting to ask him. He was perfectly prosaic about it.

'I can't really tell you, John. I don't know. But when it happens I get hunches, unmistakable sensations down in my solar plexus, which tell me I'm wanted. I always had it with my mother. I knew when she wanted me or was in trouble, things like that. But it isn't two way traffic. I can't send much back, if you see what I mean. When I'm down there, among them, then I can more or less pick up their thoughts, get the drift of it anyway . . . but they aren't thoughts like you hear in words, it's . . . it's knowing what's meant really . . . that's as near as I can get to it. For instance, this time, I know they expect us, expect you . . .'

'I'm certainly looking forward to it.'

'You seem to have endeared yourself to them in some way - perhaps just to the girls!' and Peter turned to smile at me. 'You see, their senses are very highly developed. They see things, hear things I never see. They're so much "all there" they don't miss anything. They seem to know your mood, what you need, before you do yourself! They can tell from your back view just how you're feeling. It's uncanny. You can't pretend to them with words as we all do all the time. It's how you are that matters - and that they know, just as clearly as they see you.'

'It's frightening! But how wonderful - if we could bear to put all our cards on the table like that!'

'If, if, if! I know I'm covering up all the time!' Peter laughed. We drove on to the airport in silence.

I expected to be excited at going back to the island. But the sight of it was almost too much for me. I hadn't realized how deeply the place had touched me. Peter came at the island another way and I had hardly recognized the peak from its eastern side. Then, suddenly, I saw that it was smoking.

'Good God, what's that?' I ejaculated.

I think Peter was surprised too. 'Maybe that's their worry. It's happened before. I told you. Remember? It seems to open up a fissure, sort of safety valve. Quiets down in a week or two.'

'Let's hope so.'

We swung out over the estuary and round the point to see the long dark shore. It was glorious. I felt again all the excitement and promise of our first landing. But this time it was no empty beach, no 'desert island'; there was a group of men, evidently waiting for us. How did they know? They ran to surround the plane as we rolled to rest.

They sang, almost shouted, a tumultuous chorus of welcome as Peter opened the door. We both jumped down on the sand. There were the usual double hand-shakes all round as they seized what little luggage we had. Then Peter loosened the wing roots and folded them back onto the body. Four of the boys pushed the aircraft up from the sand into the shade of the trees.

'Out of sight and out of sun!' was his comment. 'They always do it.'

Meanwhile I had to disengage myself from a man sized hug from Roka. 'Where is Sibu?' I asked.

'Sibu! Sibu!' he laughed, remembering clearly I had no doubt my first hilarious initiation into the effects of those loveshells. Then he jerked his head up hill as much as to say 'Sibu is there.'

Together we all climbed the little hill to be greeted by Pili who flung her arms round me, felt my back, my sides, sniffed my neck and gave my hair a tug and then abandoned me to Sibu, turning away to greet Peter and the others. Sibu stood aside, eyes cast down, looking so beautiful and demure, I could hardly reconcile her with the voracious man-eater of our first encounter. But when she looked up almost shyly there was no mis-taking the look in her eyes and the implications of reaching for my hand. She was as appetizing as a ripe peach - and she knew it. (And so did I!)

It was Peter who stopped me being lured away into Sibu's arms by saying, to that young lady's obvious disappointment, that we must first visit Theo and the Elders to find out what had made them call Peter down so urgently. Perhaps they needed us. And he smiled at me: 'Sibu must wait!'

So we set off together across the isthmus towards the palm plantations and the pavilion dell. Several young men accompanied us on our walk and, as we passed people's homes, the children came running to offer Peter garlands of flowers. Soon he was loaded and I took some from him.

'Looks like you've just won a Gold!' I laughed.

'I never can get used to it. I shall use them to decorate the Elders. I wonder if it would throw them?' The idea seemed to amuse him, but not having met the Elders I couldn't quite see why.

At the entrance to the dell, the young men escorting us faded out. The dell was a woman's area and that day it was a scene of almost frenzied activity. A sort of spring cleaning was going on. Teams of women in each pavilion were washing, sweeping, scrubbing, repairing. They all seemed wholly concerned with their work and at the same time I kept catching phrases of song as they went about it. It all had a ring of happiness about it. But what a contrast to the last time I had been here! Then the accent had all been on ease and indolence, surrounding the young mothers with love. Now . . .

'They're getting ready for the next batch,' observed Peter.

'What about the lot that have to be cleared out?' I asked. 'What happens to them?'

'Oh, they'll be all right, busy settling their kids in with foster parents, suckling the ones that aren't quite weaned, weeping a bit, I expect; but they'll settle down. Don't be sentimental, John. This is a very pragmatic community, you know. Nobody's left out. The mothers

81

will always be honoured for having been mothers. They just move on, that's all.'

We walked on past the dell along a broad path that seemed to be better tended than others and began to lead us slowly up the slopes at the base of the mountain. Below us on the left I noticed a long low roof, as if several of their little huts had been put together end on end.

'That looks quite a big place. What is it, Peter?'

'Oh, haven't you seen it? That's their hospital. Let's call in on them.'

We turned down towards the place, which looked out on a fairly wide open space where the trees and thick vegetation had been cleared. The building was really only a roof and a floor, like all the other houses I had seen here, but it seemed to have been carefully placed to catch the breezes. As we came closer I could see mats, some of them padded with kapok, laid out at intervals, with people of different ages and sexes lying on them. In the middle was a sort of central dispensing area with baskets and bowls of various sizes filled with leaves, powders, salves and so on. It all had a quite sophisticated and organized air about it and the girls, whom I took to be nurses, moved among their patients as if they knew what they were doing.

But there all formality ended. The patients were all surrounded by friends, relations, children and the mat of every sick person was thick with flowers. So there was a quiet bustle of activity everywhere, though nobody as far as I could see was dangerously ill. Everybody seemed overjoyed that we had come to visit and made a great fuss of Peter, taking his hands, rubbing his arms and generally fondling him as if he were some beloved family pet. Then, as usual, their spontaneous singing broke out. It was wonderful for me to hear it again and I found myself, suddenly, quite overcome by the purity and simplicity of people who could so easily catch the passing moment and give it like a flower to those they loved.

'Is it a general hospital?' I asked Peter.' I mean none of these people seems seriously ill. Is there another place for those who are really sick?'

'No. This place is big enough to look after everything. But, as I told you, there's very little illness. Most of these people are here for breakages, sprains, cuts and so on. That woman over there is having a broken leg set. The girl by her mat has put her into a hypnotic trance. She feels nothing now; and of course she'll be heavily sedated when she comes round.'

'Are there many who have these powers?' I asked him.

'I don't really know. There are certainly "doctors" with remarkable powers of diagnosis, who can "see" without probes or microscopes, so to speak. They understand touching too. It's amazing how much they can get from just running their hands over you. Perhaps that's how it was in the old days at Epidaurus! Everybody understands relaxation and massage. They have different kinds of humming for inducing sleep, soothing pain and so on and all the children are taught how to recognize herbs and roots and leaves and the uses they can be put to. But as to hypnotism, mesmerism and all that, I know they have these powers, but finally you have to leave it at that. The main thing is that people on the whole are wonderfully fit. So they must understand the health business pretty well.'

'That's all very well, Peter. But what happens when people are really ill? Something that requires major surgery - heart or kidney failure, cancers, compound fractures. When you hear how people were treated in the old days, it makes you thank God for the blessings of modern surgery.'

'All I can tell you is what I've observed. First, it's quite surprising how little illness there is. That's due to the lifestyle, I suppose. I can't put figures to it; but I've an idea that an enormous percentage of medical effort today goes into treating a whole range of 'civilized' diseases which grow from the sort of lives we lead, from our nervous tensions, lack of exercise, overeating, office routine and general laziness - to say nothing of the people who only imagine they are ill.'

'But there must be times when it's a question of life or death, when, here, there's nothing to be done.'

'When people are dying you mean?'

'Yes, dying. When modern surgery or modern drugs might save them.'

'This is the hardest question, John. Theo teaches that it is a matter of destiny. You are born with an allotted span to experience, learn or suffer certain things. What matters is how you meet them. If you are kept alive for a few years when your powers are really damaged or used up, does it help? Have we some unknown spiritual destiny outside time? People are outraged by this, of course. Saving life has become a mania, impossible to question. But the quality of the life saved, that's another question. We never look at that.'

'You mean we don't understand the purpose of life.'

'Of course. The Buddha said "Work out your own salvation with diligence." I don't think one can take it much further. We are passers-by, confronted with a mystery. Look! Great men have founded great religions, made great conquests, built great civilizations - all without the aid of modern medicine! Today's great men are pygmies! Minimen! Worshipping the mechanical civilization they've invented!'

Peter laughed abruptly, shook his head and, after a pause, went on 'But there's one thing I can tell you about this island, John. They know all about painkillers, sedatives, anaesthetics and so on. When death is inevitable, the departure of their friends is always made easy, peaceful and surrounded by love. Since death is inevitable for all of us, I don't see we can ask much more than that.' He broke off. 'But we could talk about this all night. Let's get on up and see what Theo wants.'

I would have liked to have stayed much longer. There was such an air of restfulness and contentment about the place, I felt people must get well here. But Peter wanted to get on, so, rather reluctantly, I followed him and we resumed our walk. The broad pathway climbed steeply, circling the mountain.

We were not alone. Nobody seemed to be coming down, but there were a few people, men and women, walking up with us. Among them were some who did not seem to be dressed, or rather undressed, like the others. They wore light coats down to the knee, not fastened, but loose to the breeze. Usually these coats were yellow in colour and so were the light turbans they wore round their heads. They seemed preoccupied and did not greet us, as most others did, when they passed.

'Who are these people?' I asked Peter. 'They look different.'

'They are dancers or musicians under training. They are a bit different from the rest. They have different food, I believe, and have certain disciplines and restrictions. I don't really know what their training is, and I don't want to appear curious about something that is evidently sacred to them. But, broadly, as I understand it, from these people come the future Elders. They are not chosen, I believe. They choose themselves by offering themselves for this special kind of life.'

'Funny. I've always felt the island ruled itself by a sort of natural good sense.'

'It does, more or less. But there are certain attitudes, certain principles, which need to be renewed from time

85

to time. Somebody has to take this responsibility for the good of all. Most religions have such principles. It gives people somebody to refer to.'

'But that means having an élite, Peter. My old Dad used to say that all corruption comes from having an élite.'

'Maybe. But these are simple people and they need someone to respect. Anyway, it seems to work and that's the great thing. You know, John, I sometimes feel the ordinary rules don't apply here. The place is unique.' He broke off with a short laugh. 'But of course another part of me insists it's just an oddity that Theo happened to find, a curiosity to the anthropologist, bound to be swept away, forgotten, sooner or later.'

'I don't believe that, Peter.' I found myself on the defensive. 'I think it may have some special purpose.'

'And when that's been worked out, whatever it may be, the whole island will suddenly disappear. Pouf! Just like that!'

'If its purpose has been worked out, why not?'

It was a fanciful idea and I laughed with Peter at the thought of some magician's wand wafting the whole island into eternity. Yet, in quite another way, I did see what he meant. There was something so incredible about the place. The deep blue of the ocean, crashing on the rocks below (for much of the coast was not protected by reefs), the necklace of foam, the emeralds and sapphires of the shallows, the dark border of the sands, all this seen from our pathway, as it climbed higher and higher, circling the mountain, was set off against the luxuriant foliage of forests, palms, shrubs and flowering trees, a whole palette of greens that made the island glitter like a jewel in the sunlight. Contrasting it all against the drab overcast skies of the UK it seemed overloaded with life and I could well yield to Peter's fantasy that such a marvel might suddenly explode and disappear - it was all too good to be true.

We had made a complete circuit of the mountain before we came to the temple. We came upon it suddenly at a turn in the path and it was breathtaking. It wasn't really a temple at all, just an open level space, a giant step as you might say, cut into the steep slopes of the mountain. In shape it was roughly circular and had a low wall or parapet all round the edge. It seemed to hang sheer above the ocean a thousand feet below and, standing back, you looked out over an infinite horizon of sky and sea and felt you might be floating on some disc set on the lip of the world.

The floor of this temple terrace seemed to be sand, perfectly level and even, big enough to hold at least a thousand people. There were no decorations or ornaments anywhere to be seen. Only nine cubes of black stone, carefully dressed and similar in size, stood at what looked like nine points round some imaginary circle whose centre was also that of the temple itself.

The stark emptiness and severity of this lonely eminence had a powerful effect on all who came there and there were many appearing in twos and threes, as if for some evening ceremony. They stood back from the terrace on a slight incline rising between it and the mountain side that seemed to be a sort of viewing area to watch everything that went on.

Peter and I stood, like many others who had arrived, transfixed by the magic of the place.

'It is here that the big ceremonies of the whole island take place and the daily dances and prayers at sunrise and sunset are held here too.'

I nodded and after a moment Peter turned to lead the way towards a rough archway over a path that disappeared to somewhere higher up the mountain.

'This is the way to the place I call the "Elder's Lair,"' Peter laughed. 'They hold their conferences up here -

and I believe Theo's quarters are around here somewhere, but I've never seen them. Nor where the Elders
or students live either.'

After a few hundred yards we came upon a small
terrace, also set in a magnificent position, with a palm-
leaf roof shelter shading a part of it, snuggly set against
the mountain. Here, too, were seven of those black
stone cubes set on a circle.

There were several old men, some standing looking
at the view, others seated on one or other of those black
cubes, who, as soon as they saw us, came forward to
greet us. I now saw there were six of them. They all gave
us the usual hearty double handshake and without more
ado seated themselves on six of the stones. Peter, who
evidently knew the form, seated himself crosslegged on
the ground behind the seventh stone and made signs for
me to sit by his side.

Theo must have come out from somewhere behind
us, for I was not aware of his presence till he sat on the
empty stone immediately to my right. I should never
have recognized him as the impressive robed figure I
had seen on the beach a week before. Wearing nothing
but a loin cloth, his back (which was all I could see of
him) showed the unmistakable marks of wasting and old
age, only the carriage of his head and the stillness of his
bearing gave the immediate sensation of being in the
presence of 'something' - though I could not have said
what it was. He joined our silence and at once gave it
depth and meaning, though what that meaning might be
I had not the slightest idea.

Then began the strangest conference I have ever
attended. Nobody moved. Dead silence reigned and
after looking at each of the old men in turn and
admiring the calm, inward-looking peace in their
features, I began to wonder what, if anything, would
happen next. Nothing did. It seemed that nothing ever

would. Time had come to a standstill. I heard a drum beating far below in the distance. A bird called. Then absolute silence again. But now it seemed to begin to work on me. I felt a sort of inner force building up between us. Perhaps if I 'listened', so to speak, to this silence I should understand what it was all about. But of course that was all imagination. I neither knew nor understood anything. I felt myself a tolerated outsider in the presence of something strange and powerful, but what it was I knew I should never understand.

At length some slight movement among the Elders made me realize that the meeting, if such it could be called, was over. Peter turned to me.

'As far as I'm able to understand them, it seems they are expecting trouble. Some kind of dispute, threat maybe . . . And there was something else I didn't get . . . But they think it's serious. They want to avoid violence and asked if we would speak for them, act as inter-mediaries, smooth things over and so on . . . I tried to let them understand we would do what we could - if we were here. They seemed quite certain we would be. Is it okay by you?'

I nodded and he turned to Theo and said something in Greek. Theo nodded and rose and all the Elders with him. He then turned to me and, as our eyes met, I had a sudden clutch at my solar plexus and such an extra-ordinary feeling of love and awe for this waif of an old man, who, by his very presence, seemed to expect the devotion he evoked and who would return it a hundred-fold. His firm double handshake made me tremble, but he smiled it all off and made a gesture that we should precede him down the path towards the temple below.

CHAPTER TEN

When we got down to the temple terrace I was surprised to see how many people had gathered there, standing on the slight rise behind the terrace itself. They were all very collected and quiet, as if expecting something.

'Is there going to be some ceremony?' I asked Peter.

'Every evening at sundown there is the island's equivalent of vespers,' Peter replied, and then after a pause he went on. 'Theo began it. He taught them that all life comes from the sun and that we all have a little sun inside us. These two lights call to one another. The fire of life is in all of us, we have only to bring it out. So if your life is, so to speak, sunlit, you can never come to much harm. They seem to have put all this into the form of a dance, which renews the wish in them and brings them back to their source.'

As he spoke, the dancers, who had been standing in a group nearby, walked out to take their places. All the rest of us came closer to the rim of the terrace, standing behind Theo and the Elders.

The dancers - there were nine of them, all men - took up their positions, each standing on one of the nine black stones which, as I have said, seemed to form the perimeter of some imaginary circle that was the heart of the temple. The sight of these young men standing there in their pale yellow turbans and cloaks, open to the knee, perfectly composed and still, statuesque against the evening sky, somehow caught me off guard and a shiver of emotion - I don't know what - love, sorrow, longing - ran up my spine. When they turned to face the sun and slowly raised their arms in supplication, high and wide, they seemed to me, for a long moment, eternal, and caught me up into a euphoria I had never felt before. They lowered their arms like a sigh and stepped down from their pedestals, turned inwards to face each other and at the first drumbeat, the dance began.

I really cannot describe it, though it seemed, to begin with, simple and the movements very precise, keeping time exactly with the drum. A moment later, the sound of two gourds being tapped together could be heard. It sounded almost disembodied, remote, its rhythm overlaying the drum and complicating the beat. Against this, a steadily mounting intensity of feeling was building up in those young men. The pace quickened, the pattern became more complex as they moved backwards and forwards, turned on themselves, raised and lowered their arms, turned their heads, all evidently to a long-studied and clearly defined design.

Finally the dance seemed to reach a sort of plateau of intense emotion and stayed there. The assembled company, caught up in it, began a low soft humming on a single note, as if the note was the dance, as if the movements themselves had become music. Harmonics seemed to be added and the repetitive movements of the dancers became almost hypnotic. Bathed in the glowing gold of the setting sun, the scene was transformed, sacred, so that all who saw it seemed filled with awe at some heavenly perfection of which they knew but never could find.

All this, utterly unexpected and, as it were, super-imposed on the simple life of the island, left me at a loss, moved, bewildered at the contradiction. This was a new way to give thanks, a new way to pray. Then, simply as it had begun, the dance ended. Theo, the Elders and those mysterious young men disappeared up the mountain while the rest of us moved down in the short twilight. Before we reached the beaches it was dark.

We had both been too much moved by all this to talk. Pili and Roka gave us something to eat when we got down to the coast and later we strolled up to the hilltop looking down over the estuary. The moon was rising. It was very beautiful.

'I feel a bit bewildered, Peter. Out of my depth. At first I thought these people were simple, warm-hearted savages; but very soon I began to feel something else. I found I was happy - without knowing why! Everything delighted and excited me. There was something absolutely different about it. At first their silences frightened me; but then, as I began to accept them, I saw it was what made them so relaxed, gave them that quiet, steady look of contentment and, well . . . I began to love them. But now! This evening. That dance, or prayer, or anthem, or whatever it was - it was so moving - a new way to worship! What are we in the presence of, Peter? It's another world, a sort of Shambala!'

'Not quite that, I think.' Peter spoke slowly. 'I don't know much about Shambala. Wasn't it supposed to be a sort of holy city, a congregation of saints, or something? The island isn't that. It certainly is "out of this world" as we say, but at the same time quite pragmatic. Theo loved these people he once told me because, without knowing how, they had found a practical way to live. "My children," he said, "have understood the two streams."'

'The two streams?'

'Yes. He said that people are divided into two streams. One stream lives to serve God, the other to serve Life. The Life servers are the big majority; but they need the inspiration of the God servers. The God servers are a tiny minority, but they point the way to the

Life servers. Both streams are necessary, each sustains the other, needs the other. When both are strong and true you get this wonderful atmosphere. We saw it very clearly this evening. Those young dancers were born and bred on the island; but they felt called to another way of life. When young people, boys or girls, have this need, they come to Theo and he trains them to try to live it. What they give back to us inspires us to reach, for a moment, a level of understanding we could not reach without them. So, when there's a near perfect balance, as there is here, people live in another state - near perfect society.'

'And it's unbelievable!'

'Yes. That's our problem. If it gets known it becomes a curiosity. Food for the media. If it remains unknown, it's no help to anybody.'

'But has it got to help anybody?' I protested. 'Let it exist as it exists! I've always believed there are unknown powers that direct human destiny. Perhaps they make these experiments, these jumps - a sort of kink in the DNA. Sometimes they work, get established, some-times they die out. I don't want it all dissected, Peter. I just thank God for it! I want it left alone!'

'So do I.'

We lapsed into silence, busy with our thoughts. Then Peter happened to look up. 'Unfortunately,' he said slowly, 'there are people who don't.'

He pointed and I saw the silhouette of a small ship sliding into the estuary. It looked like a seagoing vessel with a wheelhouse and funnel up forrad, something like a tug. But aft it had been decked and fitted out with cabins. A government vessel probably, some naval or police patrol boat, going round the islands, making surveys, counting heads, imposing taxes and so on. What would they want? It was not going to be easy to see them off. But the boat did not seem to be armed.

She dropped her anchor, the sound of her engine ceased, only her nav lights showed. All was quiet on board. She lay in the lee of the offshore island that guarded the estuary and the fishing nets. It looked as if she had put in for the night and we should have to wait for any signs of life till the morning.

We heard a short signal on the drums, distant, and a moment later Roka appeared. He was followed after a short time by four of the Elders and after them, Theo himself. There followed another of those mysterious, silent meetings, interspersed every now and then by a word or two between Peter and me. The upshot of it was that he and Roka and I would keep watch throughout the night, in case there was any movement on the boat. Next morning a dozen or so of our young men would meet our visitors there on the shore when they landed. We would see if they were armed and find out what they wanted. Our team of dart-blowers would be hidden in the trees nearby. Peter and I would not appear unless there were difficulties. It was when nobody answered their questions that we thought problems might arise.

Peter and I settled down under the trees. The night was warm and still. The moon serene above it all. Roka would keep the first watch. I dropped off to sleep.

The sun was well up before the first signs of movement were seen aboard the boat. A man came out of one of the cabins, yawning and rubbing his eyes. He was soon followed by another, and another, till six men were stretching, scratching themselves, clearing their throats and spitting over the rail. After a few moments and a word or two of conversation, they went about their duties. One of them, the cook I suppose, went below to brew up coffee, another drew up a bucket of water and began to sluice the decks. The others went inside again and a moment later a seventh man, whom I took to be the captain, came out of the wheelhouse, he was dressed in white shorts and shirt, wore a white-topped military style of cap and carried a revolver in its holster on a belt round his waist. He gave some order to the one man left on deck and disappeared into the wheelhouse again.

The man lowered a dinghy into the water and brought it to the companion way. After another long pause the captain reappeared. Four men were evidently going with him. Two carried short carbines, the other two, leather briefcases, which, we thought, probably held papers on which to set down the results of their examination of the local inhabitants. They got into the boat.

Peter and I made a hurried detour down to the stream and, crossing it, went into the trees and moved along the shore to where it seemed most likely the dinghy would land. Half a dozen of the island's young men stood waiting on the beach near the trees. Behind them four others remained in the shadows, their tubes and darts ready. They were to make no move to help the boat to beach, and simply wait for any sign of hostility. They were not to use their darts unless the intruders attacked them.

As the dinghy neared the shore, one of the crew, crouching in the bows, jumped into the water and hauled the boat up onto the sand, the other three jumped ashore and pulled the boat up further. The captain, sitting in the back, then got to his feet and stepped out without getting his feet wet.

He was a short, stumpy, pompous-looking little man and he walked up to our people and greeted them with a smile, speaking in Spanish. The young men bowed, smiling gravely, but of course did not answer.

The captain then began to reel off questions and when he got no answers, he tried again in English and then in other native languages and dialects. Our young men remained perfectly calm, smiling from time to time, but seemed to understand nothing. Seeing that the captain was not getting anywhere, the sailors joined in, trying other dialects and slang phrases. But nothing evoked the least response.

At first this seemed to amuse the sailors. They found it funny that these stone age savages could not understand anything, probably had some language of their own that nobody had ever heard of. They had never met anything like it before. Here was their captain, who always pretended to know everything, obviously quite at a loss and this amused them too.

But it did not amuse the captain. He didn't like his own men laughing at him. He didn't like getting apparently superior smiles from natives. He was being made a fool of. These idiots could perfectly well answer him, if they chose, but if not . . . He flushed, gave an order and drew his revolver. The other two armed men brought their carbines to the ready.

'Now,' he covered a boy, Talu, in front of him, 'don't play any more games with me. You understand me perfectly well, don't you?' Talu smiled and bowed slightly. 'Very well. First I want to know how many people live on this island. So fetch your chief here to talk with me.'

Talu was frightened. He pointed to his breast. 'Talu,' he said.

'I don't give a damn what your bloody name is!' The captain exploded, flourishing his gun. 'Go and get your boss man, and bring him here, double quick!'

Talu suddenly turned and bolted for the trees. The captain fired. Talu fell. The other lads rushed for safety, the sailors firing at them. It all happened in a split second. Only our dart blowers kept their heads. The captain and the other two carrying guns were all hit in the neck or face. They swooned away at once, falling to the ground. The other two with their briefcases didn't know what had happened. They looked round wildly, stooping over their fallen comrades. Two more darts found their marks and they too fell. In a moment, it seemed, Talu was dead and lying with the five other men on the sand.

As soon as we saw the danger, Peter and I had started to run to the rescue. But we were too late. We fell as we ran, for, as if to orchestrate the event, at that very moment, we were thrown off our feet. We had been running under the trees, and I thought I must have tripped over something, but when I saw Peter sprawled beside me and felt, at the same moment, the whole earth lifting under me, as if it was about to burst and fall apart and saw the flash and heard the roar of the eruption above us, I knew what it was to be caught in an earthquake. At the same moment the mountain top seemed to burst apart. There was a terrifying fan of flame. Rocks and smoke were spewed high in the air. We just held our breath, lying there, waiting for we knew not what to happen. It was a moment that seemed to last for ever. And then, just as suddenly, it was all over. There was a great gust of wind, clouds of angry black smoke whirled away; but the earth was solid beneath us, we were still alive. We lay there, stunned for a moment by the sudden fury of the event.

When we picked ourselves up and looked round there were flames in the sky and a golden rain of tiny white hot particles was falling on us. It was incandescent dust from the eruption drifting down. It looked most beautiful and I felt certain it would set the whole island on fire, but, strangely, as it reached the ground, it went out. Then I smelt the smoke and heard the forest trees snapping like pistol shots as the lava boiled over them. But the eruption had stopped. Clouds of smoke darkened the sky as they drifted away. There was a strangled roar of burning forest as if the earth itself was groaning under the lava. The crisis was over. Slowly we began to come to and remember where we were.

I picked myself up and began to think about sorting things out. I saw Peter bending over Talu, lifting his limp arm and letting go again. I saw the four dart blowers pulling the darts out of their victims and starting to drag the bodies into the shade of the trees.

Then Theo appeared as he always seemed to do when he was needed. He stood for a long moment over the fallen Talu and then Peter and I lifted his body and carried him under the trees. I felt sure his 'family' would soon arrive to do what had to be done. Peter learned from Theo that two other boys were wounded, luckily not seriously, one in the arm, the other in the buttocks. They were both on their way to the hospital. There remained the problem of our five prisoners and how to get them and their boat away from the island.

I had quite forgotten that there were two men still left aboard the boat. They were leaning over the rail. They had heard the shots, seen one of our men fall, swiftly followed by all four of their own mates and the captain. At the same moment the volcano had burst over them. Above them they could see the lava and the smoke still pouring from the mountain. What had happened? Was it the eruption that had caused the death of their friends? At any moment they expected the volcano to erupt again. Terrified, all they wanted was to get away. They shouted and made frantic signs to us, seeing us as strangers among the islanders and no doubt hoping we could help them.

I cupped my hands to my mouth and called out over the water. 'Hang on. Coming.'

There was no answer. Peter repeated what I had said in Spanish. 'You must come and get your mates,' he added.

Neither of them seemed to understand. Peter went back to Theo and they stood together silently for a moment or two. Then Peter came back to me.

'I'll give you a hand to launch the dinghy. We'd better row over to them.'

As I was rowing across, Peter said, 'Better stand off a bit and talk. They might easily turn nasty.'

When we got nearer I lay on my oars and Peter hailed them in Spanish. He told them we were tourists who happened to be visiting the island. The captain had murdered one of the natives and his brothers had replied with curari darts. This didn't seem to matter to them. They didn't give a damn about the others. All they wanted was to get away; but they didn't know how to work the boat. They were frantic, hysterical. Peter quieted them by explaining that the poison was not lethal. It was a drug, which had put the others to sleep. They would wake up in a few hours. But it would be better to get them back on board. These people might want to take the captain hostage. With them it was a life for a life. But we had some influence on the island. We could guarantee them safety. When they were all safely back on board the captain, when he woke up, could decide what to do.

The idea of actually going ashore themselves, was the last thing these two wretches wanted to do. But Peter pacified them. They need never leave the boat. We would see that their mates were brought to them and they could then simply row them back on board.

So, finally they agreed, if one of us would remain with them in the boat. Peter assured them that he would. So at last they came down the companion way, sat rather anxiously in the stern and we rowed ashore.

Peter was as good as his word. When the boat nosed up on to the sand, I jumped out and hauled it up a bit more; but he continued to sit with the two men. Two of the islanders appeared carrying one of the sailors and carefully laid him in the bottom of the boat. They returned to the trees and a moment later came back carrying a second man. It was a big dinghy, but by the time all five were laid on board, the boat was heavily laden. Peter suggested they should all three get out to lighten the load and turn it round. So they all stepped into the water and attempted to float the boat, but it was still too heavy. Seeing this, two more natives appeared, offering to help, and I admired the way, as they came up behind to push, they deftly planted a dart into the back of the neck of the two men and saved them, when they swooned, from falling into the water.

Theo stood watching the last two men loaded aboard and came to the side of the boat and looked long and steadily at its seven-man cargo. Then, as if dismissing the whole thing with a wave of his hand, he summoned others who materialized out of the trees, floated the boat and began to swim with it across the estuary.

It was quite a tricky job, when they were alongside, getting the heavy bodies up on deck; but when it was done they signalled to us to come over. It turned out they wanted our help in getting the captain into his own cabin and choosing berths for the others. So we swam over and got it organized, wondering what would be their next move. It was simple. Two big canoes appeared. With Peter's help on the working of the winch, the anchor was got up, lines from the canoes were made fast and, leaving one man aboard to cast these off later, the canoes started towing the boat out to sea. Peter and I dived off the stern and swam ashore.

'How far will they take her?' I asked Peter. 'Won't she drift ashore again somewhere?'

'They know the currents,' Peter replied. 'She'll just float around for a couple of hours until they begin to wake up. Then they'll wonder what's happened, shake their heads and set course for their base, wherever that is.'

It was not until much later I realized the way Theo waved away the dinghy with those people aboard exactly expressed the importance he attached to the whole incident. Compared with the murder of one of his own people and the fitting burial that must follow, it was nothing.

Before we swam ashore after seeing the intruders towed off, Talu's family had tenderly washed the blood from his body and placed him on a sort of stretcher. Four men lifted him and, with Theo and the Elders at its head, we all began a slow procession along the shore. The whole island, of course, knew what had happened and soon there were many people following the bier, which was surrounded by those who had been closest to him in life. Everybody, young and old, seemed to wish to bring him flowers and soon his body was quite hidden under them.

By the time we caught up with them, the mourners had reached a point beyond the little island that protected the estuary and had laid the body on the sand. The mood of the singing that floated along with the crowd was sombre and it continued as all of us filed past Talu, his beautiful young face very calm and composed. Some of the women knelt to kiss him. Others just laid hands on him. There was no hysteria of wailing or weeping. All their grief could be heard in the singing which seemed to be taken up by groups in turn as they felt their feelings rising in their throats and I thought I had never felt the sadness of parting and the mystery of death so deeply.

Meanwhile they had lifted Talu and placed him on another big mat, a stone beneath his head. Other heavy stones were added and the mat was folded over his body and firmly bound with cords. When all was completed, the body was carried into the shallows and placed across the outrigger of a canoe which had been brought alongside. All this was quickly and expertly done since all the island's dead were buried at sea in this way. Many walked into the water to put their flowers on the slim golden sheath and the two men at the paddles waited for a sign from Theo. When he raised his hand the singing stopped and the whole company fell to their knees and remained in silence for a long moment. Then Theo lowered his hand and the canoe moved out, fighting the breaking swells, until it reached smoother water. Then one of the men in the canoe raised his paddle while the other released the cords. As Talu plunged into the blue water, all those on the shore rose, raised their hands high above their heads and burst into an outburst of valediction, a glorious wave of farewell and then turned to embrace one another.

But Theo had turned to face the mountain above us. He stood for a long moment looking up at it. It was as if he were coming to some decision. The island had to be turned away from its grieving and he knew the means of doing it. A murmur began to run through the crowd. He was telling them of something that had to be done. A complete change of mood surged up in everyone about us. Suddenly he made a long high shout. At once, to my astonishment, everybody dispersed hurriedly as if there was a lot to do. Roka beckoned and Peter went off with him.

Theo and the Elders walked away from the shore up towards the stream and the pavilion dell, the entrance to which seemed to be the place where everything happened. I followed them, mystified. Something was afoot, but it was not till later I understood that the men had been sent to make up the long torches, cut from bamboo and soaked in palm oil, which they used to light their way when they had to move about at night.

These preparations took some time and it was late afternoon before the men began to come back. They crowded round Theo. He seemed to choose among them, passing something very special. Then, with a shout, half a dozen of them turned from him and began to run up the path which led to the temple and the peak of the mountain above. The rest moved off as if they also had something to do. I had watched all this, caught up in the excitement which seemed to have infected the whole island. When Peter turned up with Roka, he carried an extra torch in his hand, which he gave to me. He was sweating with exertion.

'Well,' he said, 'I never thought I should live to see this!'

'See what?' I thought we'd all seen about enough for one day.

'Bringing down the fire! There's an old, old tradition, coming from God knows where in their subconscious, which tells them that the fire in the heart of man is somehow connected with the fire in the heart of the earth itself. It is every man's duty to keep this fire alive in his own hearth and never allow it to go out.'

'Well, Roka certainly never lets his fire go out,' I said. 'I've noticed that.'

'None of them do. It's a funny thing in a hot climate like this. Some sort of superstition, or myth if you like, tells them that the connection between man's fire and the earth's fire must never be broken. But the story goes deeper than that. It says that man's little fire gradually loses its life and every so often must be renewed. But, for this renewal, they have to wait till the earth is ready to give it to them. The eruption was the signal that the moment had come. So now the women will put out all the fires, make new hearths and every family will meet to celebrate bringing down the new fire!'

'It's a great honour, and a great danger, to go up to the very heart of the fire and, lighting torches from it, bring it down to relight every hearth on the island. The boys may get caught in the intense heat and burn to death. Last time, it is said, they lost two. So now the whole community is in a state of deep anxiety for their young men.'

Now we could see, in the glow of the sunset, many men and women, carrying torches, all hurrying towards the pathway to the temple above. Peter and I followed. 'I'm sure that's where they'll wait,' he said.

By the time we got up there it was already dark and the glow of the lava was like a wound in the sky. Many were on the terrace already and, at every moment, others arrived to stand with them. All carried their unlit torches and were, like us, looking anxiously upwards. Roka, Pili, Sibu and Riri found us and stood nearby. The tension mounted every minute we waited.

At last someone cried out at the sight of a flickering flame way up above us. It could only be one of the boys coming down the mountainside. A shout of joy burst from the throat of everyone on the terrace. The first flame was followed by others and the excitement grew as the boys came tumbling down, panting and exhausted, bringing back the fire.

Everyone rushed at them to light their torches. Roka took his from one of the boys and we all pressed round him, taking our fire from him. I took mine from Sibu. In a second it seemed the whole terrace was afire with a hundred flames. Suddenly a sort of spontaneous madness overcame us all. The whole community started to dance round the temple together, our torches making a great turning wheel of light. The stamp of our feet and the chant of joy which burst from our throats sounded more like a series of orchestrated shouts than music, but there could be no doubt about the joy it celebrated. Then, after that moment of ecstasy, we all swirled away downhill to rekindle the family hearths. The lifegiving fire had been renewed!

CHAPTER ELEVEN

Later that evening we were all sitting round the new hearth with the family, in high spirits. The fire was burning brightly. Pili, with a sudden sly wink, brought out a gourd of so-called wine. I think perhaps it was supposed to be kept for special feast days. Well, this was certainly a special feast. The Fire had been renewed. The eruption had subsided and those murderers had been towed well out to sea and left to get out of their mess as best they could.

'Good riddance! We shan't see them again.' Peter summed it up; but I couldn't help wondering: would they find their way back?

Sibu had been sitting by me, filling my gourd and looking after me so demurely that Pili was laughing and Peter, who didn't miss much, joined in.

'She's in love with you, John. Lucky man!'

I felt myself blushing. Sibu had certainly grabbed me that first morning and the sudden violence of it had touched something in me that had never been touched before. It was wonderful and I was proud - though I had done nothing to be proud of. I had just run away - but I knew I wanted to hold on to her. I wanted to feel what I had felt again and again.

But, whether it was the drink or the fact that we'd had practically no sleep for twenty-four hours, I was yawning and I saw that Peter was too. The others would have been happy to celebrate all night. But they saw how it was with us and, laughingly, pretty well carried us to bed. I hung on to Sibu; but I was asleep before she kissed me.

She woke me next morning shortly after dawn with such warm endearing touches, fawning on me with crooning sounds and soft rubbings and kissings all mixed up, doing things for which there was clearly no need of words. But it rapidly brought me to a state that satisfied her expectations. Still only half awake, I was happy just to lie there and let things happen and, in a blissful, half-dreaming wonder, to surrender to scents and tastes and the slow-building rhythms of her supple flesh which quickly gained on me. Soon I had woken up, no longer content to let her ride me, and violently rolled her over. An intoxicating desire to master her filled me. I would go on till she was enslaved, exhausted, wholly and completely mine. But she came back at me, taking my thrusts with joy, urging me to come at her again and again, crying out in ecstasy, mad to suck the life out of me and destroy me as I would destroy her.

Then it was over. Suddenly my dominating animal was dead. I was transformed and there welled up in me a deep compassionate tenderness, flooding out over this woman, almost as for a child, to enfold her, cherish her and protect her all my life. So we lay in each other's arms for a long time and slept again.

She was already at the water pipe sluicing herself all over when I joined her. She sluiced me all over too, then tipped a bowl of water over my face, threw a sponge at me and ran for the beach. When I followed she was already in the water. We splashed about a bit in the shallows together. It was all about as perfect as anything could be and only when I happened to glance back at the shore did I see Peter working away quietly on his aircraft which was still under the trees. Sibu struck out for the reef, but I came up out of the water and went to greet him. Two lads were with him, bringing bowls of water from a nearby spring and together they were just giving his aircraft what he called a 'general wash and brush up'. All four of us sat down together in the shade; but the boys, when they saw we were talking, soon moved off.

'I'm so happy I'm positively ashamed of myself!' I laughed.

'Why, for heaven's sake?'

'Oh, only my wretched puritanical background, I suppose. Sinful to enjoy things, and all that.'

'Well, forget it. There's no sin here.'

'We don't happen to have seen it, but are we kidding ourselves, Peter? Is it we who are putting these qualities on to people who are really just simple savages, marvellous, carefree, happy people; but quite unevolved, uncomplicated.'

'Uncomplicated, yes. Unevolved, I don't agree.'

'Can it all come from just having no speech? I mean your dog doesn't know what you're saying. He only hears your tone of voice, he's pleased if you're pleased, sad if you're angry. But he doesn't understand. Are these good people just that, anxious to please? How can there be anything "higher" as we call it, in such a society?'

'These people aren't "higher". They're not saints - they're not trying to be - they're just ordinary people, who are helped to keep the better parts of themselves, partly by their old traditions, partly because Theo brought them what you might call a divine injection of understanding and love - what I suppose the Church would call the love of God - and the result is about the best you can expect on earth.'

'Just a healthy, decent society you mean?'

'Isn't that what we all want? Look what we've got! Murder, torture, cruelty and violence on a worldwide scale! A thousand times more corrupt, greedy, disgusting - and lower - than anything an animal could dream of! And here, suddenly, we find something so strange, simple and good we can't believe it. And when you've watched it and shared it and gone away and thought about it, what is it that stands between their way and ours? Just speech. It's as simple as that.'

'Our precious tower of Babel!'

'Yes! It would be bad enough if the whole world had only one language; but with thousands of them! How can people ever understand one another? Add a few hundred different religions! No wonder you get chaos!'

'But, Peter, nothing can possibly change all this.'

'So it seems. But maybe Theo is right. Humanity is talking itself into death and disaster. Is this the way to get beyond it?'

I had seen Theo with some of the Elders, coming down to the beach and turning towards us. 'Well, here comes the man who's responsible for all these questions!'

Peter and I jumped up at once and went to meet him. Why was I filled with such love for this man? Just the sight of him was enough. The look in his eyes. The serenity. Nothing mattered when he was there. Or everything.

He spoke with Peter - in Greek, I suppose. When he had finished what he wanted to say, silence came again like something palpable and enveloped us all. At length Peter turned to me. 'He just came to say goodbye to us really. He grieves for the loss of Talu. He is grateful to us both for helping. He feels renewed by the Fire - and looks it too, don't you think? He hopes you will come back. He would like to see you here to stay - for as long as you like.'

I felt I wanted to thank him somehow and stepped forward. He took both my hands, looked into my eyes. 'Yasu' he said. Then he turned away with the Elders.

Quite a lot of people had followed him. They seemed sad to know we were going. They didn't know why or where to - or when we would be back - but that didn't seem to matter. ('They live for the moment,' said Peter. 'They don't "expect" anything. So they don't worry!') I felt we were sort of mascots they had grown fond of and wished us well. Some boys began to wheel out the aircraft. Sibu came up out of the sea. We looked at each other. She gave me her hands ... Suddenly the whole company burst into song. It was a send-off, a wonderful wish for good fortune, a spontaneous outpouring of love. It lifted me clean out of myself. I didn't really come to until we were airborne.

When we got back to Manila, Peter had a lot to attend to, catching up on the time he'd been away. Rosa had not yet returned from seeing her family and so, after a late supper, we sat down together to have a last talk. I had booked myself a flight to London the next day. It was quite something to be able to stretch our legs and relax after our strenuous days on the island.

'Remember how you said it was so wonderful to get away from the rat race of city life, Peter? Come and relax on a desert island, you said! Well . . .'

'I must say I didn't think I'd be letting you in for all that; but it's been exciting all the same.'

'My dear Peter, I wouldn't have missed it for worlds! It's been the most exciting, wonderful weekend I ever had in my life.'

'Yes,' Peter was musing. 'But would the novelty wear off? Would it last? Should we die of boredom? I know I should. I find it all refreshing, stimulating. It interests me; but I can look at it from the outside. I'm not engaged. I don't want to live that life. I've got Rosa and my own life. I couldn't stand living there permanently.'

'I feel I'd like to try it, Peter. Seriously, I mean. The

only snag is my inquisitive brain - always pondering and questioning things.'

'Of course. That's the snag. That's the way our civilization has developed. To live there you'd have to drop all that, learn to communicate the way they do - passing ideas by thought. It isn't easy; but I'm sure you could get into the everyday side of the life here: but would it be enough? Or are you really looking for something more?'

'I feel I want to get to the heart of the whole thing.'

'I don't think you can get there by thinking about it, being inquisitive. The ambition of the head isn't enough. Only the ambition of the heart leads to heaven. It looks like the simple life - but it isn't.'

'And we're too sophisticated for the simple life?' I saw his point.

'In a way, yes. There's a lot to be said for the simple life. It's the way God has made it, after all. To search for your soul isn't an educational requirement! Maybe the heart of all your longing is to be found on the island, John - if you want it enough . . . After all, Theo wasn't an ordinary man. He came half round the world searching for . . . something. What he found was fertile, healthy ground in which something more could germinate. The life-as-it-is side was wonderful. He left it as it was, only giving it a little help to grow . . .

'Adding to it, you mean?'

'Yes. Bit by bit. Their natural state was a heaven-sent gift on which to build because he felt sure that among all the simplicity and purity, he would be sure to find a few, a tiny minority (which was all he needed), who were looking for something beyond themselves, the "unknown certainty" as it has been called, and these he might be able to help and guide in their search.'

'So you mean there's a sort of school for Elders there?'

'I suppose you could call it that.'

'And what is taught?'

Peter paused for some time before answering. 'I don't think you can reduce it to words. You might call it the eternal contradiction - to struggle towards a life of selflessness in order to find yourself - and then to try to pass that on.'

'But how?'

'By your presence. By your being. You saw that sacred dance the other evening?'

'Wonderful!'

'Yes. Every pose, every gesture we make, as I understand it, is an unconscious echo of the way we are. If people who know how to put a series of postures together in a certain order and in a certain rhythm it will arouse, in those who watch it, feelings, longings, aspirations which will direct them towards God - in just the same way as musical melodies and harmonies can do. You saw the effect of the sunset prayers. All this helps these good people maintain their wonderful state and that's a sort of feedback to the Elders and their pupils to increase their efforts to care for and watch over them. It's this extraordinary two-way traffic that makes the island what it is.'

All this had given me plenty to think about and we sat together in silence for some time.

'Life on two levels,' I said at last.

'Yes, that's what it comes to. The higher level becomes quite sterile, introspective, if it only looks inward and the lower level degenerates at once if it loses all sense of direction - as it has today. Theo talked a lot about balance, harmony. He used to say that in the West people only think about educating their heads. If you suggest they educate their feelings they don't know what you're talking about. Here, on the island, the emphasis is all on feelings, values, on how to refer things to your conscience ... All far stronger than thoughts. It isn't that these people haven't got heads. They have. But they haven't had them turned into a mill of nonsense, thank God, by talking themselves into this technological madhouse the world is so proud of. So here there's the beginnings of harmony. You can see it, feel it, that's why there's hope, I think.'

Again we were silent, thinking.

'I feel the need,' I was musing aloud, 'to be joined to something bigger, deeper, than my ordinary life ...'

'To get out of the kitchen - and go upstairs!'

'Yes. I suppose you could put it like that.'

As usual, Peter helped me not to take myself too seriously. 'I'll tell you what I'd like to do,' I went on, 'I'd like to try and get back here for the Festival of the First Spring Days. When is it, by the way?'

'The first week in May, roughly.'

'Then if I still feel the same about it all, I'd like to get closer to the island - permanently - somehow.'

'Well, it's a big decision. See how you feel about it compared with the UK. If you want to come back, let me know.'

So it was agreed and next morning I left for London.

There is no place like an aeroplane for thinking things out. For a few hours you are free from the past and the future, suspended in a sort of vacuum where you can take an almost detached view of what has happened and what you think may happen, sort things out and see your way ahead.

My casual impulse to break my trip out to Australia via Manila had led to such an extraordinary feast of impressions, it was only now it was over that I began to realize how much it had turned my life upside down. I had blithely set off on an exciting desert island weekend only to find myself involved in a set of experiences that were so bizarre and improbable that nobody would believe me if I told them what had happened to me.

And beyond the instant happiness of setting foot in an earthly paradise, there were these deeper overtones, calling to hidden sources in my life which had been buried, blunted and almost discarded under the veneer of everyday, but had now unexpectedly come up boldly, very much alive, demanding answers to questions that have no answer.

So, slipping off my shoes, tipping my seat back and closing my eyes, I settled down to try to sort things out. I realized how far I had come since my first visit to the island. Then, I had been mystified and excited by something strange and different about the 'natives' - as I thought of them then - but soon came that sharp flash of excitement and wonder when I felt that somehow or other they communicated with each other without speech. That was the first real shock. It put them into quite a different category. These people had no speech! It was inconceivable, impossible: but there it was. And somehow they seemed to do quite well without it.

Speech, after all, was a faculty, something you acquired by copying, like riding a bicycle or threading a needle. I remembered that poor boy who had been brought up by wolves and rescued by well meaning people who tried to coax him back to humanity. It couldn't be done. It was too late to teach him to speak. That part of the brain was atrophied. He died.

Something like that must have happened to the island. Human beings had existed on the earth for millions of years. While they were just another creature, their strange faculty of speech didn't matter. It was when people began to imagine they were lords of creation that the trouble started.

As I'd slowly begun to accustom myself to these ideas, I'd rationalized it by seeing them as just very simple primitive people, only a step above the animals. But that didn't fit with that strange group of questioning figures, or the wonderful singing, or the open, trusting way they were with one another. In fact the more I saw of the way they lived and got to know their customs, their dances, their ceremonies, the less and less did they seem undeveloped, simple. This was another sort of simplicity . . .

Yes! The idea was suddenly there in my head - it wasn't the simplicity of ignorance, of savagery, it was the simplicity of a deeply evolved society, far beyond anything our so-called civilized, sophisticated world had got to. These people were way beyond us.

Suddenly seeing this was like a sort of inner explosion, a flash of insight, as if I had been initiated into another way of thinking, feeling, behaving, as if I was made over anew. And with it came a flood of joy, of understanding, of humility at having had the chance to be shown this possibility, this hope, for myself, for others, for the world.

There must have been a crossroads, way back when primitive man had come down from the trees. There were two courses open to him: to develop through thought, or through feeling. He chose thought and slowly that way had engulfed him in a quagmire of slavery to words. The island had somehow chosen the other way, to develop feelings and refer everything to them. Only now, when we had come to realize the failure of thought to help our evolution, were we beginning to see we had made a bad choice. Could we revert to the way of the heart?

I felt I had been given a glimpse of the far distant future, into a time when people had finally struggled free from the morass of their own slavery to greed and ignorance and found a way to harmony and happiness.

To have stumbled on the island was miracle enough,

but to have seen that such a life existed, to have had the chance to take part in it, even maybe to return to it, what right had I to all this? How could I deserve it, preserve it? Clearly it was hanging by a hair, almost any serious intrusion could destroy it. It was like a child's cry in a thunderstorm and filled me with a longing . . . for what? For the dream that was long in coming, for the hope so often deferred, for the rest our labours deserve, for the heaven our hearts long for, for perfection in this life . . .

The note of the engines changed. We were coming down.

I never bother to let Sybil know exactly when I'll be home. Planes are not always punctual and its quite a trek down to our little place near Dorking. So I opened the front door, glad to be back and even looking forward to seeing Sybil in a friendly sort of way. But the house was empty. A few letters on the hall table, no heating on and, when I got to the kitchen, nothing in the fridge. No signs that the house was inhabited at all really. So I dumped my things, turned on the central heating, the hot water and the radiator in the sitting room and sat down. I was tired after the long flight and had looked forward to a hot bath and supper. But clearly that was not on, so I picked up the mail, mostly bills, and as the room warmed up, must have dozed off a bit.

I woke to hear Sybil's voice outside. A man answered. A car drove off and a moment later Sybil's key turned in the lock and she came in.

'When did you get back?'

'A couple of hours ago.'

'Have a good trip?'

'Fine. Thanks.'

She was looking fit and fresh, took off her raincoat, warmed her hands at the fire and lit a cigarette.

'I'm afraid there's nothing in the house. I've had supper. I didn't expect you.'

'Of course not. I had a meal on the plane. I'll just have a hot bath and turn in.'

She sat. 'I've taken up golf.'

'You look fit.'

'I like it. The exercise suits me.'

'How's your mother?'

'Fine. You're a week later than you said. Any trouble?'

'No. The Sydney thing was postponed. I went to the Philippines.'

'Interesting?'

'Not bad.'

We really had nothing to say to one another. I got up. 'Well, I'll have a bath and turn in.'

As I went out of the room, she said, 'By the way, I've had the beds altered. I thought we'd find two more comfortable than one. Hope that's all right.'

'Good idea,' I said and closed the door.

As I lay in my bath, I guessed that something had happened to Sybil since I was away. Changing our double bed for twin beds summed it up very neatly. It didn't touch me in the least. What else could I expect? As a husband I had practically no experience of sex. In my own family it was never mentioned and nobody had ever told me 'the facts of life'. So I was gauche and shy, while Sybil, though perfectly willing to discharge her wifely duties, wasn't much help, because, it seemed to me, she wasn't interested. I had hoped that with time it would get better, but it didn't and I suppose we both felt somehow frustrated, because it ought to have been wonderful and wasn't.

It happened that just then I got a step up in the office and my job began to be far more interesting and demanding. I worked long hours, came back late and our home became little more than a dormitory. Sybil didn't seem to mind. She was glad I was doing well because that meant more money, her own car and all that. I suppose it's quite a usual routine, but it left me feeling nervy, short-tempered, cheated. I promised myself that one day I'd cut loose. But somehow or other the opportunity never came up. I don't fancy tarts and nothing much else is on offer when you travel as much as I do.

Peter had said I'd see the whole thing in a new perspective when I got back and I shouldn't make up my mind about anything in a hurry. But I must say my first reaction to coming home was a violent longing to get back to the island. But making a complete break was going to need a good deal of practical planning. So I took Peter's advice to give everything a chance, said nothing to Sybil and went back to the office to see how things stood there.

They were better than I'd hoped. The Sydney conference had been a big success, judging by our order book, and the directors were pleased. But there was a lot of work following it all up and I found myself engulfed in all the details of office routine. I was able to put up with it much better than before I went away because now I had an aim, somehow or other to develop our contacts in the Philippines, and get out there to set it all up in the spring.

I thought the best way was to tell my bosses that I had been very impressed with the possibilities there and thought they seemed worth further investigation. It was too early to think of setting up an office, but we might be able to appoint a suitable agent and, if things went well, develop from there. So I proposed returning to Manila in the spring to tour the major islands, get a better idea of local conditions and make a full report.

On the strength of my success in Sydney, there was

no opposition to the idea. The project was agreed and I began to get down to dates, routes and bookings. Much nearer the time I said I had friends in Manila and asked if the firm would object to my taking a fortnight of my annual leave while I was out there. Certainly, they said; but I must without fail, be back for the annual general meeting to be held early in May, to speak on our Far East developments.

I wrote to Peter, telling him what I had arranged and asking him to confirm that my dates were about right. I also told him that my feelings had not changed since I got back and that I felt more and more strongly that I must get back to the island. But, at the same time, to give myself a last chance, I proposed to say nothing to the firm or to my wife until I had finally decided, come back to the UK to report on the trip and, if I felt as I thought I would, wind up all my affairs and decide to emigrate permanently. His reply was laconic: 'Fair enough. Give me your ETA.'

To Sybil I said nothing. As far as she was concerned it was just another trip abroad. She continued to be more and more taken up with her golf. (Or with her golfer, I thought to myself, since she took care to be so well turned out when she went to the club.) But I was glad for her to have found this new interest and if it turned out to be with somebody who suited her better than I did, then that would be a happy solution for us both. So, with everything arranged and Peter warned, I took off for Manila on the last day of April.

CHAPTER TWELVE

I was glad to find Peter waiting for me at the airport. While we were waiting for my luggage to come through, I asked him for news of the island. After three months I was excited to be back. His replies were rather vague. He hadn't been down there: but he'd had several 'messages'. There was evidently something troubling the people; but exactly what it was he couldn't make out. Now I'd come, we'd make a quick trip down there together.

As we drove into town I told him what I'd arranged with the firm and how much time I'd got. He gave me the date of the Spring Festival and it looked as though that would give me about a week in Manila to look into the firm's business and, with luck, to set up the ground work for further investigation and development. Peter knew a lot of people in the city and had several contacts he thought would help. In spite of the long journey I felt full of energy. It came, I am sure, from the excitement of getting back. So I went up to Peter's flat, paid my respects to Rosa, had a shower and then, grateful for the heat after the rigours of the UK, took a siesta which lasted till supper time. I was far more whacked by the journey than I'd thought.

I devoted the next few days to business, taking care to leave the way open for someone else to carry on my work, if I decided to chuck it. That done, for the moment at least, I went to a travel agent to check on my return flight, got a firm booking of date and time and then, with a feeling of freedom at having done my duty, couldn't wait to get to the island. We escaped from Rosa with Peter's usual excuse that he must get in the air to clear his head and cool off. When we were airborne he took a roundabout route, having almost an obsession about being tracked by radar. 'We must keep the place from being discovered,' he said.

My heart rose at seeing the island again. I didn't think it would move me so much, but it was more exciting and glorious than it had been the first time. There wasn't a sign of smoke from the mountain and the radiant lights on the sea dazzled me with wonder.

Quite a lot of people came hurrying down to the shore to meet us, clearly expecting us to go up to Roka and Pili; but Peter wasn't staying overnight and wanted to be back before dark and made it clear he must pay his respects to Theo. He thought I should do so too. So we set out to climb up to the temple to find him.

He was sitting alone on one of the stone blocks in the place Peter called the Lair. He evidently knew of our arrival and expected us. As he got up to greet us, I saw, for the first time, the power and serenity in his face, the steady deep look in his eyes, telling me in some strange but certain way that no lies could exist before him. We stood there in silence. I do not know what he was passing to Peter, but to me came an immense sense of love and pity. I felt he was carrying the life of the whole community in that frail frame and would bear it stubbornly and faithfully to whatever end was in store for him and it. I felt a deep wish to help and, at the same time, that all help was useless. The intensity of feeling that came from him filled me, but it was too much. I knew I could not live at that level and was almost glad when he dismissed us with a warm sorrowful look and we could go.

'I feel he is carrying too much,' I said as we walked down the hill.

'He always does. But now I feel he knows he has to face some situation beyond him and that gives him his tragic look.' Peter sounded very disturbed.

'What can it be?'

'Maybe his death. Maybe the fate of these good people without him. I don't know.'

'Not much we can do about that.'

'We can give him support and love - that's all.'

'I felt he was terribly alone.'

Peter nodded. 'We all are, when it comes to the crunch.'

We walked silently down the hill and, when they saw Peter was leaving, many people seemed sad and came down to the shore. I asked him to leave me here as long as possible and he promised to come and get me a day or two before I had to go. That would give me about a fortnight. But I begged him at the same time not to be late. I mustn't on any account miss my London booking, out of loyalty to the firm after all they had done for me - even if they didn't know it!

Peter laughed. 'You'll probably be sick to death of the place before then!'

He climbed into the cockpit and when they knew he was going there came from all the islanders' throats that spontaneous outburst of love and sadness at parting which I always found so moving. It seemed a reminder of how fragile everything is. We watched the aircraft disappear out of sight.

It was only now that Peter had gone I felt I was actually here, on the island. I had looked forward to it all those winter months in the UK. Now it was real and I had the feeling of belonging the way I'd always dreamed of. To be with these people and take part in their life for all of two weeks made me feel like a resident. The days stretched ahead. I could relax and enjoy everything without the feeling that in a moment it would all be over.

Of course Sibu had a lot to do with it. How often on those lonely evenings back in the empty house had I thought of her! I saw that I had really never had any youth. During the permissive years of indiscretions and excesses I had been so much inhibited by my strict and sterile upbringing that I had really never known what it was to enjoy anything. I was ashamed of sex and even the freedom of marriage had failed. I had never let go.

But now, because of Sibu, I had suddenly woken up to a sense of virility and manhood I had never known before and with it, I suppose, a greediness to make up for lost time. Sibu encouraged me. She certainly suffered from no inhibitions whatever and indeed welcomed me and urged me to feed my starved appetite and enjoy her in every way as much as I enjoyed myself. The result of all this was that I remember almost nothing of the preparations which were then coming to a head to celebrate the 'annual orgy' as Peter and I called it - the Festival of the First Spring Days.

It was not until we came out of our own private orgy that I realized to what extent the island took the coming festival seriously. Everybody was simply bubbling with excitement and anticipation. Everywhere you could see groups of people, young and old, busily inventing and making up their costumes. Usually working in twos and threes, they were helping each other, trying on this, altering that and showing off each bit as it was completed. Headdresses, necklaces of flowers, feathers, seeds or shells, were worn in striking contrasts. I only realized later that, as they were made to be worn at night - and then only by fire and torchlight - how all the violent colour would be toned down. Besides these personal costumes, there were troups, men and women, all wearing similar fantasy gear. Parading and exhibiting all this and competing to show off their inventiveness and skill filled the days. To top it off there were the nuts, who took this yearly opportunity to show off their eccentric individualities or pornographic quirks.

The setting for the festival was the site of those grotesque straw figures I had seen on my first visit to the island. Now they had disappeared and the place turned into a sort of primitive arena. The open slope with its backdrop of trees made a natural stage and in front of it a row of footlights had been made by setting hollow bamboos into the ground and filling them with palm oil and kapok wicks. They burned with a smoky flame, but it was enough, with other bigger torches at either side, to light the performers.

There was nothing subtle about the night's entertainment. The public - that is the whole population of the island - when they weren't taking part in the dances themselves, sat about near the footlights helping themselves to the special 'wine' which, as I have said, was only brewed on this occasion. They drank from big gourds of it which they liberally handed round and this, coupled with the throb of the drums, rapidly loosened up the party.

Before sunset things had already started to get under way. You could feel the tensions rising. People were parading up and down, showing off gorgeous costumes in the glow of a golden evening. The effects were so fantastic, bizarre, and wonderful that no contrived effects on stage or screen could begin to compete with them. Then, as the light went, fires and torches began to be lit. The stage was set and the throb of drums welcomed the dancers.

Decked out like cockatoos with great masks of beaks and feathers, a line of young men strutted out of the shadows. Their bellies, circled with targets of red and white rings, proudly centred on those natural bullseyes which, as they flourished them in the dance, soon began to draw cries of delight and anticipation from the elderly ladies, reminding them of things they had long since almost ceased to enjoy.

When these had finally stamped themselves to a standstill, they broke up and joined the spectators to give way to another lighter nimbler set of drummers who ushered in a ravishing chorus line, parading their costumes like peacocks. Short kilts of coloured leaves hung from their waists which in the whirl of the dance flew up to display enticing vistas, while their natural beauties, bobbing and curtseying in the torchlight made an exciting contrast to their huge, enticing eyes, smiling with promise. Such beauties, crowned with haloes of white or crimson feathers, dazzled the men who began grunting and groaning with approval. Finally, when the wild rhythm had swirled to its climax, these houris minced up to the 'footlights' and, with legs apart, flexed their knees, thrust forward their bellies and with a gesture of superb abandon pulled aside their girdles of leaves.

The effect of this was to unleash a sudden over-powering sexual urge in all present. You could feel it running through the company like fire. With a roar, the men stampeded to get at the girls and, whipped up by the wine, a general tournament began, on stage and off. Costumes, abandoned or torn aside, flew in all directions. Ecstatic cries and the wonderful heaving surge of coupling and thrusting filled the air. In the flickering firelight I thought I had never seen anything so mad and so free. Sibu, coming up out of the shadows, dressed only in a crown of flowers evidently thought so too and, rousing me to immediate action, pulled me down on top of her and our rising tide of desire rushed headlong to its climax, till we lay (like everyone else) in a daze of exhausted silent satisfaction.

The whole place grew quiet, full of love breathing, and after some time two men emerged to fuel the fires and straighten the torches knocked askew during the excitement. Then the drums started rolling to announce an interval for rest and recuperation and the tumblers bounced on. Compared with the sophistication of the West, their somersaults and handsprings were simple enough, but to the island they were marvels of magical skill and the wild abandon and headlong rush of their routines set the spectators shouting and clapping with pleasure and astonishment. When they had finally catapulted themselves out of the torchlight there was hardly a pause before a roar of applause and welcome heralded the entrance of the clowns.

There were two of them, most comically contrasted. I called them Venus and Adonis. Adonis was a small, thin, perky little man and a born comedian. He was ridiculously, but seriously, determined to seduce the lady of his choice, a Venus of noble dimensions and a particularly ample backside. Playing the audience with every sort of saucy and suggestive gesture, Adonis approached his Venus slowly. Humbly, politely and slyly he sidled up to her - and then suddenly faced her to reveal his 'equipment' which was miserably thin, small and painted blue. He proudly displayed it, turning it this way and that, inordinately pleased with its beauty. However his Venus, after a mock gasp of wonder, having doubts perhaps as to its efficacy, leant forward to examine it more closely and then, with a gesture of disdain and disgust, tore it off him and threw it away!

With a yell of anguish, Adonis, holding himself, rushed off, while the crowd roared its delight. His paramour, sadly disappointed at being abandoned and at losing a pleasure to which, in general she was so much addicted, seated herself dejectedly on the ground, and then, attracted by some flower, knelt to examine it more closely.

Adonis, reappearing at this moment, hopeful as ever, could hardly believe his eyes on seeing such ripe appetizing goodies on offer. But Venus was no chick in the art of self defence. She disdained the shouts warning her to beware of an assailant. So when Adonis rushed her, seizing her hips and driving up her, she was equal to the situation. Unexpectedly ducking into a forward somersault, she took her man with her, and the pair, to everyone's astonishment, surfaced, having completed the circle, in exactly the same position.

At this the crowd fell about. They had never seen anything so funny in their lives. After two or three repeats of this cartwheel love, Adonis got off his Venus, slapped her backside and made his exit, giving us a warning gesture of a surprise to come. Venus, to show off, walked on her hands, swinging her legs into astonishing positions and only righted herself in time to see her Adonis return with a shout, holding a torch in one hand and in the other displaying the most enormous erection which had somehow or other sprouted from his loins and was painted bright red. This wonder he waved about to the wild ecstasy of his Venus. She came nearer to worship it, whereupon Adonis lowered his torch and ignited the tip of this gigantic prick. It spurted fire. Venus ran off screaming, pursued by her inamorato, aflame with love. It was a long time before the crowd stopped shouting its delight.

Everybody had, of course, plied me with drink, with the result that I passed out before the orgy really began. Any hopes of rivalling Don Juan slid away into sleep and the dawn had come before I woke with an awful head and lurched down to the shore to sober up in the healing sea.

It took the island about two days to recover from the festival. The jousting had continued throughout the night and among the younger and more abandoned, after a brief sleep, was rekindled at sunrise. But soon after, it gently died and then everyone retired to sleep it off.

Then began what were for me the most perfect and beautiful days of my life. I do not understand why or how it happened. There were, after all, none of the usual wonders that make a honeymoon. Sibu and I had no common hopes or dreams to share, no memories to amuse us, no endearing love talk to light up our intimacy. Yet this intimacy and understanding was so complete it did not seem to need any of these embellishments. We began to find out what we enjoyed together. There was the island to explore. We walked and climbed it, bay by bay and valley by valley. We reached the peak, still hot underfoot from the last embers of the eruption. We smelt the sulphurous stink of the air still escaping from the cracks, saw the black tongue of lava creeping down towards the sea, felt something awful in the power the earth could unleash. Sibu did not like the desolation and the dark thoughts it engendered. She shuddered and clung on to me, hiding her head in my neck, and then ran on ahead down the slopes and did not let me catch up with her till we were safe in the canopy of trees below.

There, she was quickly consoled with many touchings and feelings and clingings together and we walked on hand in hand. Her simplicity and purity seemed to lie only in the realm of her affections. She punctuated our silences with her own little personal cry or call quite often, making the four notes gay or plaintive, changing key or dropping into the minor if she was sad, so that I always knew her mood. But all the time she was very attentive, very alert. She found flowers in the undergrowth I never should have seen, picked fruit for us to eat, pulled down blossoms for their scent and put them in her hair and in mine. At every sudden view she stopped and looked and invited me to stop and look too, in long moments of sustained wonder. It seemed she wanted to share everything with me and me with everything. She could imitate the calls of birds and bring them close to us before they found her out. Then she would clap her hands and send them off, screeching.

As the days went by I felt I began to understand the way she thought, but not the thoughts themselves. All this was hidden from me. But all the time I felt there was another sort of life going on inside her. I began to see it in the way her friends turned up. Girls of her own age would appear and sit with us as if they were expected. Then she would show me off, pinch my arms, run her hands up my thighs and invite her friend to do it too. If I withdrew or protested it was an occasion for laughter, but it did not stop them doing it! I suppose I was always a sort of curio to them. My pale skin and fair hair, my size, much bigger than their own men, and my strange cries - which though they were speech to me were just noises to them - all this I am sure intrigued and excited them. Sibu wanted to share me with them, as she had shared everything with others all her life.

I became quite sure she could 'call' her friends because, on another occasion when we were already making love, one of her friends appeared. I would have stopped and disengaged myself, but I was on my back and Sibu - it was her favourite position - was riding me gently as she loved to do. The visitor, a most beautiful creature, came to sit beside Sibu as naturally and easily as if she had just dropped in for tea. The two girls exchanged looks, evidently of admiration at me, and Sibu, as if to show me off, rose on me and sank back, a movement she knew I could not help replying to. Repeating this, in a way she knew very well how to do, soon made me forget there was anyone else there. I closed my eyes in bliss, but opened them a few moments later in amazement to feel Sibu sliding off me and her friend deftly and expertly taking her place. I was too astonished to protest and Luzi (for that turned out to be her name) came down on me and began to ravish me with her kisses and her jasmine-scented hair, settling me more deeply into her. Quite dazed by all these changing emotions, I turned my head to look for Sibu, to find her looking lovingly at me and gently stroking Luzi's tail, urging her on, obviously enjoying the other girl's pleasure.

All of this, which would have shocked me out of my wits a month ago, now seemed to me, though it surprised me, no more than the custom of the country. So we remained a little while. I felt perfectly at ease in this strange triangular situation, but Luzi began to grow restless, her loins pressing, urging, her desires rising in her. Suddenly she sat up, exchanged a glance with Sibu, who understood and at once leaned forward to reach my mouth. Deep in my kisses with her I felt Luzi's slow movements quicken and tremble. When she gasped I came, seizing Sibu's head, and madly smothering her with kisses . . .

When I woke up, only Sibu was there. I took her deep in my arms, closer to her than I had ever been.

Already since my arrival there had been at least one earth tremor, a slight quake which many people did not even notice. But on the third day, we had a really scaring one. A sudden sideways jolt flung us all to the ground, the mountain roared and erupted, rocks were shot out into the sea, clouds of black smoke arose and then, just as suddenly, it was all over.

But evidently the disaster posed by an eruption on a bigger scale was often uppermost in the minds of Theo and the Elders and they had made preparations for it. I happened to be on the beach when I felt the quake and was alarmed when I heard a moment later, confused cries coming, it seemed, from all over the island. These grew closer and seemed to focus on the small bay where Peter had shown me that fleet of boats. I ran along the beach to reach the place and when I got past the point, was amazed to see the whole population of the island standing round the boats.

Evidently some order had been given to everyone to arrange themselves, so many men, women and children to each boat. All the Elders were there and it seemed it was they who were organizing the thing, but there was a good deal of confusion and it was quite some time before they got it all sorted out. This, it seemed to me, must have been their first try out and when it was over they all stood in silence, while, as I thought, they were being asked to remember their positions and come to them at once if the order was given. Then the whole company faded away. An hour later you would never have known that anything so important had ever happened.

But the whole thing started me thinking. Was it a plan to save everybody if the island blew up? Would there be time? How would they know when they had to go? Eruptions could start as this one had done and just subside or they could blow the whole place up. And where would they go? How would they find the sort of destination suitable for the life they wanted to lead? They knew nothing of the outside world. And the weather? Now it was perfect, but if what I had heard was true it could be stormy and very dangerous.

All this went round and round in my head, but of course it got me nowhere. It only left me worried. Typical! As I went about among them all, I saw it didn't trouble them in the least. I laughed to myself when I saw exactly what would have happened if people had been able to discuss it! The endless debates about procedure, organization, priorities. This was a perfect example of the virtue of silence. The island accepted the fact: this might happen. If it did, this is what they would do. But until it did, it played no part whatever in their lives. Their serenity was perfect, marvellous.

Almost every morning during the days I was there, Sibu awakened me before dawn, splashed water over my face and hers and led me up the mountains to join in the dawn prayers. I think it was particularly important to her at this time before the great marriage ceremonies. Life on the island was about to be renewed and she was part of it and so came with her silence. I was glad to be with her in this and everything. I had found a new valuation of life. Everything on the island was so rich, I felt so open, so alive, I walked on air. I kept saying to myself: I've fallen in love. I'm deeply in love - with a creature of another race. We understand one another in a way that doesn't depend on all the props of civilization. It rests on something deeper, some interplay of body and spirit, which I don't understand. All I know is I need these prayers as much as she does. There she was now, at my side, hand under my elbow, guiding me from time to time to keep me on the dark path, as we climbed the broad pathway and came on to the temple terrace.

The place looked huge and ghostly white in the first glints of dawn. I could just make out the shapes of others collected there, a group of women whom I knew by their long tunics to be dancers, and with them the Elders and many of us 'ordinary' people come to take part in the ceremony.

The dancers were facing the dawn, kneeling in a shallow crescent. It looked as if they had breastplates of gold and backs of steel. Then, as they rose and started to make those movements, which looked so simple and inevitable and which I was quite unable to remember afterwards, the light began to roll back the night. It seemed fitting that women should pray at the birth of the day and men at its passing in this world where every sunrise was a resurrection.

I was overwhelmed by the grandeur and majesty of these tropical dawns. They came so suddenly. At one moment it was dark with only the slightest warning of a deep red glow along the eastern horizon. Then, in a sudden overwhelming uproar of golden light, our world was created!

Now the low underbreath humming that had stolen in with the prayer gained strength and assurance till it became a cry of jubilation. The dancers raised their arms high and wide, welcoming the day, and a gasp of wonder overcame me, almost like an electric shock. There was a flash of being connected with something else, strange and marvellously clear. Every leaf, every tree, every being, mountain, sky, sea, life itself, stood out with microscopic clarity, triumphant, naked to the sun. I, like the world, had been admitted to another life.

The onrush of morning swept us away down into the welcome shadows, but I knew that a drop of me had been left there in the light and, at that moment, a longing became firm in me somehow to find my way to come deeper into the life they lived on this island. Sibu looked up at me, pressing my hand. Perhaps she read my thoughts and wished it for me too. We ran down to the sea.

CHAPTER THIRTEEN

Hardly had the excitement and excesses of the Spring Festival died down than preparation for the Marriage Festival began. I noticed how the whole mood of the island had changed. There was a feeling of serious purpose abroad. This was the great yearly day of renewal.

I saw groups of people all going towards the pavilion dell, carrying flowers and decorations. Sibu showed me strange bracts of white flowers to take from big shrubs near her home and took others herself and, with arms full, we went along together. It was very different from my last visit. Round each of the little houses there was great activity. Many people were sweeping, dusting and generally spring cleaning. It was two days before the great day and the excitement was just beginning to build up. Here in this dell a new generation would be created. It was part of a deep tradition, like Easter is to us, and a joy to keep it alive.

All down the dell people were arriving, loaded with flowers with which they began to deck out the pavilions. These had already had their patchwork sides let down and strange heavy perfumes filled the little places, making them like jewelled palaces, bestrewn with cushioned beds of scented leaves. By the evening of the second day all the wealth and luxury in the world would not be their equal. On the day itself the final touches would be added and that evening the chosen ones would come. But their choosing affected the whole community, which was intimately concerned with it.

Everybody had views about those to be chosen as brides and grooms.

Although, as Peter had told me earlier, the number of couples to be married could vary with the overall population of the island, which in turn rested on last year's harvest and the food available, it had evidently been agreed that this year nine would be the number of births permitted.

But the choice had to be agreed by everybody and that made it a lengthy affair. The candidates were paraded like champions, walked up and down, carefully groomed and perfumed to be at their best, smiled at, stroked, smelt, applauded and cosseted like stars. (At one point, Riri held up a bit of the root we chewed every day and laughingly threw it away. No prophylactics for the grooms and brides!) It turned out to be fairly easy to select the last dozen of either sex, but whittling it down to the nine 'finalists' caused endless delays.

As far as the boys were concerned, the choice didn't seem to rest so much on strength or talent as on personality, vitality and style. Their looks, their physique, their general deportment, how they won or lost, all these things were taken into account - but I thought I had never seen such a splendid group of young men.

The choice of the girls was even less competitive. Their looks, of course, took pride of place, but the character, the disposition counted for much. The elderly women knew all about their domestic capacities since childhood, their competence in weaving, plaiting and in the island's herbal remedies, potions and perfumes. Their gaiety and high spirits were infectious. Seeing them as a stranger, I found each one more attractive than the last and wished I had been chosen as one of the husbands.

The island's choice at last completed, next came the

all important question of how they should pair off. I thought this would be bound to cause longer and even more violent disagreements: but I was wrong. It was a genetic matter, to be decided solely by the Elders. They took great care over it, making provisional pairings, each of which caused groans of dismay from some and subdued applause from others. They considered each couple carefully as a couple. They knew at least two generations of the island's breeding by heart, but besides this they seemed to have a sort of flair for those who might not breed well. So there were adjustments and readjustments, which sometimes caused sorrow and tears.

But finally the nine pairs stood together and for some time the whole company considered the Elders' choice. They must have come to a unanimous conclusion for, spontaneously, they burst into a long satisfied chord of approval, which rose a third and then a fifth, before dying away.

I was immensely impressed by all this. I thought how, with speech, there would have been endless argument, quarrellings and bad tempers, with elderly duennas swarming round the brides pleading their virtues and 'managers' parading the boys like stallions. But here the decisions of the Elders were unquestioned. Everything seemed to resolve itself without fuss. The mood was joyous, contented. On the chosen couples would fall the blessing of creating the next generation - sacred to them, to the island and its future. They had made it an honour to bear and to be born. The honour of creating the island's next generation had been decided.

The only thing that surprised me and, I must confess piqued me, was that Sibu had not been chosen to be one of the brides. She had not even been included in the last ten. Of course, I could have been biased, but she seemed to leave all the other girls standing. When I tried to express my annoyance at this, Sibu just looked at me and made that sweet gentle call of hers as if she did not understand.

Deep in all this, I suddenly realized, with quite a shock, that my time was almost up. Tomorrow was the day of the Marriage Ceremonies and the day after Peter would pick me up. I had now quite decided that my future lay here. Somehow or other I must join myself to the life of the island. I would just tidy up my affairs in the UK, give up my job and get back as soon as I could. Three weeks to a month would, I thought, be enough. With the help of Peter we would explain all this to Theo. He would make Sibu understand. So I intended to arrange the future.

But next morning, quite early, Theo and the Elders suddenly appeared. I jumped up to meet them and we went into the usual double handshaking that always seemed a necessary courtesy to all meetings on the island. Then there was a pause while they all conferred together, standing silently, deep in meditation. At length Theo, who was, I began to realize, a master of mime, began to convey to me in a way it was quite impossible to mistake, first that today was the day of the Weddings (which I knew), second that all the brides and grooms had been chosen; but finally - and this he did with such an elaborate show of courtesy and flattery it set me laughing - would I consider taking part in the ceremony, not as an onlooker, but as a groom. The island, he bowed, would consider it a great honour if I would consent to be the tenth bridegroom by marrying Sibu.

It took me some moments to understand what he was proposing. I simply could not believe they would allow a stranger, a foreigner, the honour of coming right into the heart of the island's life. At the same time my heart

136

began to beat wildly. It was marvellously, impossibly, wonderful. I seized Theo's hands in gratitude and love and shook them again and again. This seemed to please him and delight all the Elders enormously. They came, one by one, for a further double shaking of hands and then, without looking back, disappeared.

But Theo remained after the others had gone. He led me over to stand opposite him as he sat on the high floor of Roka's hut. He must have called Sibu, for a few moment's later she came, running. Her demeanor before him was perfect. Eyes cast down, she waited, obedient and composed, for whatever he might pass to her. So did I, though I could not know what it might be. After a little I saw two tears wandering slowly down her cheeks. She timidly took my hand. Theo, at that moment, looked serene and utterly at peace. As we stood before him, I knew he was uniting us, giving us his blessing and his hope. After a little he slowly got up, smiled on us both and walked away.

Sibu and I stood side by side, looking after him. Somehow this new bond had already altered our relationship. Our lovemaking had been a carefree exercise of intimacy and pleasure, but now I no longer felt about it as I had before. It was as if we had been dedicated to some other purpose, beyond, above us. We had responsibilities to it, to each other and to life. When I wished to take her in my arms, she let me, but stood there, quite passive, making her little call to herself, as if preoccupied with the promise of motherhood, as if she had never thought about it before.

Out of this bemused condition we were summarily awakened by another earth tremor which threw us to the ground. A deep, menacing growl made the hollow earth tremble. We waited, breathless, not daring to move. But nothing more followed. Everything was as it had been. Only, above us, we saw a plume of smoke seeping from the summit of the mountain. The volcano was warning us - though not so violently as before - stirring in its sleep again. We picked ourselves up and looked at each other, we were reprieved.

But a moment later the air above us came aloud with a whirl of strange sound. We looked up and saw the sky darkened with the beating of hundreds of pairs of wings. It was the bats. The tremor had driven them, terrified, from their cave! This had happened before, the night the boys brought down the fire; but soon they had all gone back. This time they circled, screeching violently, as if being forced to a dreadful decision. Then, in a dark cloud, they disappeared out to sea. At last their wailing cries died out. Had they left the island?

I turned to Sibu, but she hardly seemed to have noticed. Strange and troubling as it was to me, everyone on the island was used to clouds of bats leaving the cave for feeding, morning and evening. If they left at another hour today, she evidently saw nothing in it, pre-occupied, as she was, with the hours ahead. Then a few moments later Pili and Roka hurried in, laughing, pretending to fall about and shaking themselves as if caught in the tremor. They did not seem to have even noticed the exodus of the bats. They threw their arms round us both with much rough affection and then Pili, without more ado, rushed Sibu off for what I later understood to be her bridal preparations.

I understood it because Roka, with equal determin-ation and thoroughness, set about me. He stripped me and started to wash me all over (paying, I thought, quite unnecessary attention to my genitalia). Then suddenly old Kula appeared, a friend of Pili's. She was carrying a sort of gourd, full of scented oil, which she and Roka proceeded to smear all over me, rubbing it in and massaging me at the same time, till I was positively

138

reeking with the scent of frangipane.

By this time I felt so much a creature of their hands that I submitted quite passively to being fitted out with a long white coat, with which Riri had come running. It had a sort of bamboo button high in the neck, which scratched me and a plaited belt at my waist to hold the tunic together. After examining my feet, they seemed to agree that I should be allowed to keep my own leather sandals. All this completed, they stood back, looked at me, turned me round, looked at me again and I thought, rather reluctantly, considered me fit to pass as a bride-groom. Anyhow, Roka clapped me on the back, Kula grinned broadly and both of them pointed in the direction of the pavilion dell, where, I gathered, the cere-monies were to take place.

I set off across the isthmus towards the palms, but before I had gone very far I was joined by lots of other people, boys and old men, girls and matrons, going to the same direction. They were all decked out with garlands and decorated with flowers and gave me cheerful company. It was obviously an event for them to have a foreigner, a stranger, as one of the bridegrooms and they were all the time crying Sibu! Sibu! and making expressions of love and delight from which I gathered they thought me a very lucky man, a sentiment with which I heartily agreed.

It seemed that the ceremonies were to take place at the head of the dell. I saw that many people had already collected there, leaving room in their midst for the seven stools of the Elders, arranged in a line. The brides and grooms did not mix with each other, but had been shepherded aside and stood in two separate groups under the trees. The nine other boys with me were all dressed in long white coats as I was and, look-ing over to the group of brides, I saw they, too, were wearing white. Neither we nor the girls were permitted any sort of ornament. This made us stand out from all the rest, for the whole crowd, which grew larger by the minute, was a riot of colour, decked out in extravagant varieties of beautiful decorations.

As I stood there with the others, waiting, I had time to take in the whole scene. The evening was coming down. The high moon was already bringing her silver. There was an atmosphere of expectancy and joy on people's faces. A sort of magic seemed to envelop the dell below us, where the little pavilions shone gold in the evening light. It was all impossibly lovely - and I had a moment of panic, of fear. What was this world I was entering? It was something utterly different from any world I knew. The silences, the sense of being in intimate touch with magic, which to them was the stuff of everyday, the instinct that beneath the easy gentle life, lay strange powers unknown and unknowable, to me at least, all this gave me a sudden pricking up my spine. Where would it all lead me in the days to come?

What did I want? Behind all the happiness, something deeper drew me here. What was it? Not some idealistic hope of perfecting myself to sainthood. That was far too remote. Nor did I want to live with an élite so wholly focused on another world that they became aloof, feeling superior to the world they were in.

No. My hopes were more modest, more human, nearer to the sort of life that was lived on the island: a decent human life, what used to be called a godly; a righteous and sober life, not made to change, to go 'faster than God', but content to be what it was, watched over by people who had understood life more deeply, but whose ambition did not go beyond the hope that, in humility, they might be able to help those near to them to live out their lives in happiness and peace. That seemed to me a modest ambition, within human powers. Supermen who were going to change the world because they 'knew', finally led the millions they had conned into their beliefs to disillusion, war and death. We had only to look at history - and the world around us today - to see it. Our ambitions were overweening, our performance abject. Now that both sages and scientists had combined to agree on the absolute nothingness of humanity in the life of the universe, might it be possible for us, someday, to whittle our hopes down to a human scale? That alone was problem enough. Anyhow, it was enough for me.

I saw now that the Elders were taking their places. The crowd left plenty of room around them, standing in a respectful circle, waiting. Then Theo appeared and took the centre stool and, as he did so, a low humming melody of content stole out and seemed to wash over the whole company. This was the moment for the ten brides to come and stand before the Elders. They took their places before the old men and waited for us to follow. I had a ridiculous moment of comical fright - if they were not in the right order, we should all get the wrong brides! But that passed when I found Sibu at my side.

The humming stopped. There seemed to be a moment when we all should kneel. We did so, to be, as it were, bathed and enveloped in the steady gaze of Theo, the Elders and the whole company. As he sat there at the centre of this world which was largely of his making, Theo looked incredibly old, with the dignity and peace of some timeless icon. His clear eyes, his long nose, like a keel beneath the dome of his skull, his high cheekbones which might have brought an itch to the hand of Michelangelo, could you get any nearer to the image of God on earth?

A sort of anthem began. There seemed to be one group of singers who made a nucleus among the others and took the lead. It is the magic of music that a sequence of notes following one another in a loving order and rhythm can begin to create in those who hear them whatever atmosphere they will. So, at the moment of our blessing, the chorus of voices created feelings of holiness and bliss in me such as I have never known. Sibu, Theo, the Elders, the people, the whole island, were, for a moment, immortalized, perfect, beyond the reach of time.

Then silence came back. The sun had set. Theo and the Elders rose and so did we. Then from somewhere in the crowd a woman's voice burst out in a long sustained note and hung there for a moment till the whole island surged in behind it with the rush and glory of some breaking wave. The melody grew from it, swelled, was elaborated, tossed about through the crowd, changed tempo, key and rhythm as if these people used music like painting, brushing the night with such a palette of sound that it swept us all out of this world into some high place of perfection never known before, where, alas, it would die at the very moment of creation.

At last the jubilant chorus came to a close and people broke into clusters round each of the couples. Torches sputtered into life. The magic dell came alive with a rout of movement and laughter. Sibu and I, like all the other couples were hoisted onto the shoulders of our friends and carried, shoulder high, down the slope to our pavilion.

I think we were both a bit breathless with excitement and emotion when they deposited us on the cushioned floor. We clung to each other for support and this was evidently what was expected of us and raised loud exclamations of pleasure. We could see over their heads similar scenes taking place before the other pavilions. Sibu was laughing, but the tears were running down her face. In the flickering torchlight I could only see the sparkle of eyes; but I felt we were more than lovers, we were the focus of the island's hope. Then, before I could properly take it all in, someone pulled the cord of our front curtains and we were suddenly in darkness.

We fell on the cushions in each other's arms and kissed a long kiss of contentment. I started to wipe away the tears from Sibu's cheeks, while beyond our curtains we could hear low voices giving us a soft slow blessing, which died away into silence . . .

The sun was well up when I awoke to find the light streaming through our flimsy wall coverings. For a moment I did not know where I was, but then I turned to see Sibu lying at my side; her young body looked so perfect I leant to stroke her shoulder and she roused dreamily from sleep, stretched, yawned and turned to kiss me.

But these slight movements were enough to wake our friends who had been listening since dawn for the moment when we should awake. Now, with no more ado, they pulled up the hanging walls to disclose us to the world and scrambled up onto the high floor to greet us and embrace us. It was natural that they should turn first to Sibu, stroking and patting her tummy, as if to convince her and themselves that she had already conceived; but when she let them know, by their strange telepathy, how, in the night, she had felt a pang of joy, deep in her belly and clutched my hand to press down on hers and held me there and cried out loud in ecstasy, then, from their expressions and exclamations it was clear that to know this moment of conception was something miraculous, wonderful. It sent them into such a vortex of emotion, their chorus of wonder hardly rose above a whisper and we were all still.

Then, when they had recovered, they turned with equal enthusiasm on me. I must say I still found these outpourings of affection embarrassing, with all their huggings and kissings and strokings and sniffings; but today there was reason for it. Besides, I could see, across the dell, that the scene round every other pavilion was much the same. It was, in fact, very like my first visit, when I had been so moved by the crowds pressing round their friends, but they had what we had not - the newborn child to show off to the world. Well, that would come.

It seemed to be the order of the day, once these greetings were over, that everyone, brides, grooms and all their friends, should start their new lives by taking a dip in the sea. So we set off together, as happy a company as you could wish to see. Ever since Theo had blessed us I had felt a change in Sibu and the evening ceremony had made it grow. Now, knowing that she bore our child, she would not let me leave her side, hardly letting a moment go by without stopping to look at me, hold me, kiss me. I returned all this with equal ardour, to the delight of our companions, who seemed to think such public intimacy exactly as it should be.

So we came down to the shore and, choosing a point where the rollers came through a break in the reef, plunged in, splashing and ducking each other, diving through the breakers, shouting, laughing and generally gambolling about like kids. Sibu swam like a fish. Surfacing beside me, she slid up my body, hugging me in her arms and then fell back, pulling us both under water till I had to fight to get up for air. A mad moment of joy seemed to take possession of us all, a snatch of perfection . . .

And then I heard something and looked up!

It was the Cessna, coming in to land! My first thought was: damn Peter! Why does he have to turn up now? He might have given us a day. What difference does it make to him? But he was already shooting in, low over our heads, to touch down a bit further up the beach. We all - there must have been a hundred of us altogether - ran along the sand to greet him. Little Riri, faithful as ever, stopped me and handed me my shorts, knowing I did not like to go naked everywhere, and as I put them on I saw Theo coming down to the shore. I was surprised to see him there, as I ran to catch up with the others, many of them calling 'Pita! Pita!' as they ran.

Now he had got down from the plane, engines still ticking over, to be greeted by all and sundry, crowding up round him with much affection. He saw Theo and left them to go and greet him. Then he turned back and saw me with Sibu. He greeted her, 'Sibu, my dear!' throwing an arm round her shoulders, and to me 'How did it go, John? All you hoped for?'

'And more! Theo invited me to be a bridegroom and I married Sibu last night.'

'Good God!' He stopped dead, genuinely amazed and at a loss for words. At last he managed 'Sibu! Congratulations!' of which, of course, she understood nothing. She just hung on to me.

'What are you going to do, John? I can't stay.'

'Can't you?' I found I was pleading.

'Impossible. Really impossible, John. I've got all Rosa's family round my neck for lunch and a high powered delegation flying in this evening.'

'When could you get back?'

'Not for a couple of weeks, I'm afraid.'

'I must be back before that.'

'I know. I only squeezed in the trip today because I knew you had to leave.'

I suddenly felt frantic. 'Peter, understand. I'm hooked here now, absolutely hooked. It will be hell for Sibu.'

'How did you get yourself into this?'

'Peter, please! Explain to Theo. Tell him I'll be back

in three weeks - a month at most. Beg him to explain to Sibu, console her. Otherwise . . .'

But Peter was already speaking in Greek to Theo. All the people, though at a respectful distance, looked anxious at this long conversation which they didn't understand. Then, suddenly, Sibu left my side and went to Theo. As she stood there I saw her figure begin to droop. Then she ran from him, rushed at me, wrapping her arms round me, the tears suddenly pouring down her face. She was crying aloud, madly, wildly, while I just stood there, shouting, 'Only three weeks, darling, only three weeks!' knowing she could not possibly understand, feeling guilty, hopeless, dreadful, not knowing what to do.

Just as suddenly she let me go, as if resigned to losing me, stood back a pace and uttered a dreadful wail, a howl of pain as if she was mortally wounded, and fell on her knees. The women rushed to crowd round her to comfort her. Suddenly their gaze seemed to fix on me and with short angry cries, they shouted a chorus of horror and revulsion. Sibu had somehow found a stone with which she was beating herself on the head, scoring her forehead till her face was running with blood. The men began to crowd up towards me, making low furious revolted growlings. Above it all I heard a cry from Peter and, looking up, saw Theo make a quick urgent gesture. Out! Out! it said.

'Quick!' I heard Peter shout. 'They'll smash the plane.'

It was not a dignified exit. We rushed for the cabin. Peter opened up as we slammed the doors.

I must have been hysterical. I was shaking. 'My God! My God!' was all I could say. Then the tears began. An awful surge of grief took possession of me. 'Why did I leave? Why did I leave?' I kept shouting, again and again.

As we turned about to pass the beach, all we could see was the crowd round Sibu. All of them, men and women, had turned their backs on us and were crowded round Sibu, slowly, it seemed, leaving the shore. 'Oh Peter!' I cried out. 'How could I leave her? How could I? I shall never see her again!'

Peter let me cry it out. Then, much later, he said, very quietly, 'Don't worry, John. Don't worry. You'll be able to go back.'

'Never! Never!' I was speaking to myself now, sobbing uncontrollably. Then I really think I must have lost consciousness. I can't remember anything more till we were landing at Manila.

CHAPTER FOURTEEN

After two days I left Manila for London. Although I suppose I looked fairly normal outside, feelings of remorse, emptiness and despair never left me. It was the frustration, the impossibility of seeing any way in which I could right what I'd done. It haunted me. Nothing could wipe away my heartless, thoughtless stupidity. I took the grief with me everywhere, like a black cloak, all day and most of the night.

Rosa, of course, knew nothing of the island or where I so mysteriously went off to with Peter. But she must have sensed I was ill at ease and tried in her simple way to cheer me up.

'I am so glad Peter has you for a friend,' she said. 'I know you will always bring him back to me.'

Privately I wondered whether the tragedy on the island might not in fact break up everything between us; but of course I told her that I was devoted to Peter. He was my closest friend and I hoped we would grow closer because of the affection we both had for her. This evidently pleased her and she kissed me warmly when I left.

Peter, I hardly saw. He was busy, I knew, but I think he must have found the whole thing very disturbing. However, before I left we did manage to have a moment together.

'Don't make yourself ill with worry, John,' he said. 'I'm sure we shall be able to work something out. I blame it all on Theo. How could he have dreamed up such an idiotic idea? He may be a genius on the island, but he's really an idiot in other ways. It's this fixation they have about blood lines. The island is inbred. It would be valuable for them to introduce a new strain into it. I know Theo had been thinking about this. As a matter of fact he wanted to marry me off to one of the girls, but I didn't want to get involved. I don't need to tell you they're very attractive young women. But, after all, I'm married to Rosa, so I politely, but firmly refused.'

'When was this?' I asked him.

'Last year. But this time he must have persuaded the others and rushed you into it before you had time to consider what you were letting yourself in for. He saw you'd fallen for Sibu and it was exactly what the island needed. I'm sure that's why he invited you to come and stay as long as you wanted.'

'I don't give a damn about what he wanted. It's what Sibu and I want that matters.'

'Of course. It suited you - and it suited him. But how could he forget you'd be leaving?'

'It's the impossibility of explaining anything,' I said. 'Sibu lives in the moment. Now. She can't understand the future. A week, a month means nothing to her. All she knows is I've gone.'

'I blame Theo,' Peter said again. 'He understands quite well we come from another world and must return to it.'

'But he wasn't to know you'd be back so soon or that I'd have to go. Going was my decision. It's all my fault. The whole island was outraged. You could feel it.'

'I know.' Peter shook his head. 'It was a bit abrupt. But don't worry, old chap. I'm sure they'll forgive you, in the long run.' He smiled at me warmly. 'You'll get your Sibu - even if you don't deserve her!'

But on the long flight back home I found I couldn't

absolve myself so easily. I had simply, stupidly, abandoned the only woman I'd ever wanted on the day after her wedding night! How could she understand it? I couldn't understand it myself! Simply out of my slavery to a routine, to things that, compared with her needs, were absolutely trivial, I'd left her, gone! All for a ticket! What could that mean to her? And what did it mean to me? Slavery to a job I no longer wanted, slavery to the idea that I'd promised to be in London on a certain date, slavery to a purely mechanical routine. And when Peter had suddenly turned up it had never even occurred to me to break it. Being gone for three weeks, what did that matter? I'd be back. I never even thought of her needs, her distress. That terrible cry! It haunted me. It would probably make her lose her child, the child we had created only a few hours before ... And the blood running down her face! It was terrible! Terrible! How could she go back to that little house? The shame I had brought on her, to be deserted on the very first day of her marriage! The shame I had brought to the whole island, to flaunt a ceremony that was sacred to them ... All these things went round and round in my head.

But it didn't end there. I saw that I'd always taken it for granted that everything would be arranged to suit me. But not now! Not any more. Now I'd really seen how I was! Changed! Something in me had suddenly, violently, caught fire and, in a flash, I was burned for ever. It had nothing to do with reason. You could string words together all your life and never get there. I had just simply found something perfect, found Heaven, if you like - and lost it. Thrown it away - for a return ticket on an aeroplane! I arrived at Heathrow a wreck. It took me a week to recover.

I got back to an empty house and a letter on the hall table from Sybil in which she told me she had decided to leave me and that she would be marrying Jason Saunders (her golf pro) as soon as he was free. I had expected something like this, so I wrote her a note, congratulating her and asking her to let me have the name of her solicitor, so that a divorce could be arranged.

I got back into the office routine as best I could, put in a report on our prospects in the Philippines and gave details of the contacts I thought could be developed there. While I had been away the question of setting up a permanent office in Australia had been discussed and they offered me the job. It was, of course, a compliment; but I hesitated. The truth was I didn't know what to do. I didn't care. Nothing mattered. I suppose what I was really waiting for was some sign, some hope, from Peter about the island.

At the same time, I found I simply could not adjust to city life. I was almost driven mad by the deluge of chatter, of talk, talk, talk that poured over me from all sides, the dribble of empty conversation, the jabber of the media, the way we were all being driven insane by torrents of words, by the numbing torment of murder, torture, greed and corruption on all sides and the endless arguments and lies that went with them. I longed - thirsted - for the island silences, for room to let the mind flower, to meditate, to be quiet and listen to my inner world, which our 'civilization' had almost bashed out of existence.

It was about a month before I came out of this empty, wasteful state and began to get some sort of perspective. It wasn't only Sibu, though she was the bitter heart of it all, it was my fascination in the island's way of life, its unspoken philosophy, its religion - whatever exactly it was, I felt an affinity with it. I wanted to understand it, to get to the heart of it all.

So, not knowing how to begin, I started to collect

books on yoga, on Zen, on spiritualism, thought transference, Shiatzu, herbalism, anything that might help me to understand how people on the island communicated. How could you transmit thought without words? Relationships, hopes, longings, all that seemed possible; but plans, projects, anything that concerned the intellect, where would all that be without speech?

It opened up questions that were far beyond me. What was the destiny of the human race? Could we grow, get beyond this 'silly, clever' age and assume our rightful role as the Crown of the Creation? It seemed we had to find a new direction, a revaluation of all values - or destroy ourselves.

I was deep in all this when, at last, a letter came from Peter. 'Good news!' he wrote. 'Yesterday I had a "message" from the island, just as I was sitting down to lunch! Funny how these things come! Suddenly, there, in my solar plexus! Compulsive! Turning out everything else: when would I be making them another visit?

'I must say I was delighted, partly for you and partly because it meant the tie was not broken. We had not been banned for life as I feared. We could go back. So, now, John, when you've got over that, what do you want to do? If you really want to live in this part of the world, I'm just going to start on the new annexe and I could find a job for you looking after that - and other things might open up too. So let me know your ETA!'

I wired my acceptance at once - if he was serious - and got a reply the same day. Then, with a marvellous feeling of elation, I began to wind up my affairs. I told the office I would gladly accept the Sydney assignment. I rang Sybil, told her I was taking a job abroad and would be selling the house, and, in a sudden impulse of generosity, offered to make her a present of all the furniture and effects, except my personal belongings. She was obviously delighted - and it suited me very well. I didn't want to tangle with packing and sales and so on. As for the house itself, my father had made over the freehold to me just before he died. I put it in agent's hands.

But all this took much longer than I had anticipated. The delay irritated me. All I wanted was to get away. Finally everything was completed except last details: the bank, arranging credits in Manila, my passport, flight bookings - and that was it.

But fate stepped in, as it seemed to have done ever since I'd made that impulsive sidestep over from Singapore to Manila, it seemed a lifetime ago.

'Peter missing in flying accident. Please, please come at once, Rosa.'

It was so unexpected that I simply couldn't take it in. Peter. Missing! And missing almost always means killed. And Rosa! With nobody to turn to. It set my head spinning. How could it have happened? Luckily I could leave almost at once. He was such a good pilot, so careful, so safe. Was it at the island? When? Why? Round and round the questions to which there were no answers. I wired Rosa 'Coming at once' and flew into Manila three days later.

When she greeted me I thought at first that everything was under control. She was very calm, very collected and tried to make me welcome almost as if nothing had happened. I tried to play it as casually as she did, dropped my things - she insisted I had my old room - and when I'd tidied up, went back to sit with her.

I saw then how pale she was, her beautiful face drawn and thin.

'Help yourself to a whisky and pour me one,' she said.

I sat down opposite her.

'If you can bear it, tell me the details.'

'There aren't any.' Her voice was flat, almost defiant.
'How did you get the news then?'

'I never ask questions,' she began, 'I never tried to find out what he did. I always trusted him absolutely. I loved him. But when he went off in his plane, he never said where he was going or why he went. I was always frightened he wouldn't come back. That's why I was glad when you came. I didn't think you would both go off. He'd have to bring you back, whatever it was. After all, I am his wife. I have a right to know what my husband's doing, haven't I? She took a deep drink. Then, 'I suppose it was some woman?'

I might have expected it, but it was so surprising I almost laughed. I got up and took her hands. 'Rosa', I said, 'no woman had anything to do with the trips Peter and I took together. Truthfully. Put anything like that right out of your head.'

'Then where did he go all the time? Why was he so secretive? There must have been something.'

'Rosa, I'll tell you.' I had to be careful now. I knew Peter wouldn't want me to say too much. 'He happened to find an island where some very primitive, very original people lived. He was very keen on anthropology, you know; but he thought these people so special he didn't want anyone to know about them.'

'He never said anything about it to me.' She was on the defensive again.

'He never said anything to anybody. But that was all there was to it, Rosa. Truthfully. You must believe me. Don't worry about all that, my dear. It's ridiculous, it really is.' I saw from her expression it made her feel better, so I quickly changed the subject. 'Now. What I want to know are all the practical details so that I can try to help. We must make a thorough search. He may have landed on some beach with engine failure. He might not be able to get away at once. Some of these islands are pretty remote. He might have smashed the plane if he made a forced landing, then he'd have had to wait for a boat or a canoe or something to get away. I'm sure there's no reason at all to think he isn't alive and well. It's just a question of finding him. So tell me the details. When did it happen?'

'I don't know when it happened.' She was doing her best to be practical. 'Peter left me exactly a fortnight ago yesterday. He said he was just going up to the club to have a flip round. He always said things like that. Later he sent a message through the office that he'd be away for the night . . .'

'And then?'

'Then there was a sudden gale, a typhoon you might say.'

'A typhoon? There was nothing about it in our papers.'

'I don't suppose it gets into your press, but it's pretty common here in the season.'

'But there must have been a warning. He must have had a warning.'

'I suppose they thought he'd be back in time. They said he was a very good pilot. Perhaps he thought the typhoon didn't matter.'

'So that's the last you heard of him?'

'No.' She paused and I saw her control was going. 'A fishing boat came back into port after the storm, towing an aircraft wing they'd found, floating. They told the police. It had the number of Peter's aircraft on it. They'd not found anything else . . .'

She broke down then, poor child, and there was nothing I could do or say to comfort her.

I found my way up to the flying club and asked for the secretary. I told him I'd been a close friend of Peter's and had come out specially to see if there was any hope of finding him. I found he was almost as upset as I was.

'Not much, I'm afraid,' he said. 'It's a great pity. He was a bloody good pilot and an awfully decent chap.'

'He'd had the storm warning, of course?'

'Naturally, we had the cone up here. And if he was airborne he'd have had Met warnings every ten minutes. But . . . ' and he sighed, 'every year one or two people do get caught. Take a chance. Think they can make it . . .'

'I believe the wing was found quite close in. Any hope, d'you think, of recovering the body?'

'Pretty slim, I should think.' He shook his head. 'Probably sank with the plane ... and then there are sharks and things . . .'

I saw there was nothing to be done. I could give no hope to Rosa. But it wasn't easy telling her. She cried a lot at night, I think. Her eyes were so swollen in the morning. But she said little, falling back, I suppose on that fatalism that Latin blood seems to resort to in these dreadful emergencies. But she was very sweet with me. I think she knew I felt hard hit by it too.

To take her mind off all this, I asked her what she was going to do about the hotel. 'It belongs to you, I suppose?' I asked her.

'Yes,' she answered and, for the first time, I saw a little light come into her eyes. 'My brothers have a small interest in it and I suppose they'll expect to take it over - now that it's a success. No woman is supposed to be any good at anything here, except to cook and have babies. But' - and she smiled knowingly - 'I don't intend to let them. It was Peter's hotel. He didn't know much about it to start with and look what he made of it! I'm going to carry it on!'

'Good for you!' I was really delighted. I thought with her looks and even average ability, she'd be sure to make a success of it. 'I wish I could help. But I know nothing about hotels either - except that this is a very good one.'

'But didn't Peter want you out here to take over the building of the annexe?'

'That's what he said. With him at my elbow, I thought I might manage it. But now . . .'

'Couldn't you try?' she asked. 'I know Peter wanted to have you around - and so do I. I need your support to hold off the family. I know they'll be furious, but I don't care!' The defiant note had come back into her voice and I thought it was a very good thing. 'They're all down in Mindanao - and they can stay there!' Rosa was actually laughing. At that moment I knew she would be all right.

'Well,' I laughed, 'if you care to risk it, I could have a look at the plans and see if I think I can help - and if I can't I'll tell you.'

I didn't want to promise more because, of course, I wanted to get back to the island. Peter's sudden death had thrown everything else into the background. But now it looked as if Rosa would be all right, I began to let my mind dwell on how much I should enjoy seeing all those dear people again. I was deep in all this, picturing the pleasure of it, when a thought came quite casually into my mind - how was I going to get there?

The full weight of it didn't hit me right away. An aeroplane of course. I should have to hire one. Then how should I get back? It would mean the island would get known. All the complications started to spin in my head. But not until I'd thought of a dozen ways to get round all that, did I suddenly see, with a ghastly clutch of despair, the end of it all . . .

Where was the island?

I'd only flown there as a passenger. I'd never taken much notice of where we were going. I'd never flown in a small plane before. I'd just sat and admired the view of the sea from the air, quite lost my bearings of the way Peter went, couldn't understand what he was telling me about radar and just thought how beautiful it all was. The first time I was being taken to a 'desert' island, the other times I was going back to see people I longed to be with again. Getting there was Peter's job. I'd never thought about it. I didn't know a thing about map reading or navigation or anything like that. I couldn't just hire a plane and tell a pilot to fly me there. Where was there?

I looked at the map and saw that vast archipelago of islands. It made my heart sink. How could I ever find the island? Even if I could hire a plane, should I recognize it, coming at if from a different angle, a different height? I probably shouldn't recognize anything till we were pretty well down on the beach!

This sudden shock to all my hopes, so obvious once I began to think about it, nearly drove me out of my mind. I'd imagined all sorts of difficulties, with Theo, with the Elders, with Sibu, with people who might not be ready to forgive me; but this! And it was the key to everything else. Nothing else mattered.

Rosa evidently saw I was absent-minded and preoccupied and asked me if there was anything the matter. So then, feeling so dreadful about the whole thing, I told her. About Sibu, about the marriage, about my terrible, dreadful parting. How I must get back. I poured out the whole story. I must say she was awfully sympathetic. I think she must have felt an affinity with her own grief and wanted to help. Anyway she said: 'Don't think about money, John. Hire a plane, try all the likely places. I'm sure it'll turn out to be easy. There can't be so many islands like yours, with a volcano smoking. I'm sure you'll find it, John. I'm sure you will.'

Feeling a good deal cheered up, I gave her a kiss and thanked her. Then I went straight back to the secretary of the flying club and told him what I wanted.

'No problem,' he said at once. 'When would you like to go?' And he gave me details about costs and passenger insurance and things like that. 'And by the way,' he added, 'any idea of distance? Any idea how long you were in the air, how long it took to get there?'

Of course I hadn't. I said: 'Maybe two hours, three - I really don't know. I never thought of timing it.'

'Well, at 150 knots,' he laughed, 'it does make a difference! Never mind. I'll get hold of Jake and introduce you. He knows the islands pretty well. That ought to start you off, anyway.'

So next day I took off with Jake. He flew south over Mindoro. We kept the coast on our left, but nothing looked familiar to me. He swung over towards some other island. Coron, I think it was; but I saw nothing even vaguely like the island.

Jake was a nice chap and he really did want to be helpful. 'Can you give me some idea of the place? Was there a reef? Was the volcano erupting? How big was it? Any smoke?' And so on. I tried to visualize it all; but I'm not much good at descriptions. I could remember the eruptions, the smoke, the beach, the dark sands, the temple terrace, the fish nets, things like that. Jake evidently felt it pretty inadequate. We flew around for three hours or more and saw nothing that gave me the least hope. It was pretty depressing.

'How long is it since you were there?' asked Jake. 'There have been quite a number of earthquakes and eruptions. The place could have changed shape, blown up - or even disappeared. One or two islands have.'

I told him it was May when I was last there, only about three months ago. 'Well, I don't know what to suggest,' he said. 'Let me have another look at the charts, think it over and we'll have another go tomorrow.'

So we did. We went far and wide, right down to Palawan, all though the Cuyo Group, over to Panay. Nothing made sense. After four trips at about five hundred a time, I had to call a halt. I had to accept it.

I could not find the island.

It could have gone up in an eruption, of course. There had been a small one when I was there, and those repeated tremors. I had had the feeling the whole place was unstable. But could it simply vanish - and Peter with it? I just couldn't believe it. And yet, after all, he had disappeared and we never knew how or why. But that seemed such a thousand-to-one chance - and, anyway, it would have been reported, surely? Or was it that I just didn't recognize the island? Had we flown right past it? I simply couldn't accept that it wasn't still there.

The thing went round and round in my head. It was maddening, maddening. I thought I should go out of my mind with impotence and frustration. Damn it, I'd stood on the beach, swum in the sea, met all those people, been up to the temple, heard the heavenly music, taken part in the morning prayers, fallen in love with Sibu. The island was real. It was there. It couldn't have been just wiped off the map.

And then an unexpected thought came into my head: the bats had deserted the island! Just after the last eruption they had all gone! Was that an omen? It could be. And there was something else. All those boats I had seen with Peter that morning. Dozens of big seagoing craft, carefully built and cared for. At the time it seemed very strange. And all those people, knowing their places, as if preparing for some emergency. Could it be - could it possibly be - that Theo and the Elders knew in advance they would all have to go and go quickly and that strange fleet was there ready for the getaway?

Had the island been lost, but the people saved - and

Peter with them? There was a sort of impersonal hope about it that began to console me. Sibu, all those good people, were not lost, were still alive! And that wonderful way of life still existed, always would exist, somewhere ... Destroyed in one place, it would spring up in another, many others ... I could find it again, maybe ... if I deserved it - and I remembered Peter's light-hearted remark, 'You'll get your Sibu - even if you don't deserve her.' Should I? Did I deserve her? I'd reached the island, found the life I'd wanted, been welcomed into the very core of it, left my child in it - and thrown it all away! For what? When it came to the crunch, because I could not surrender to a new way of life, because I was deeply attached to all those empty things I'd sworn to leave behind me. So had I got what I deserved? Was it my destiny to be excluded?

But surely I had the right, even the duty, to close the old book before opening the new. Surely that could be understood, forgiven? Was there no mercy, no pity for being what I was?

Perhaps ... perhaps not ... Well, that's what I have to live with ...

THE
FIREBRAND
Marion Zimmer Bradley

'Still my fate: always to speak the truth, and only to be thought mad'

Kassandra, daughter of Priam the king and Hecuba the priestess, twin sister to Paris and prophetess of Apollo, her visions dismissed as lunatic ravings, is powerless to avert the fall of Troy . . .

'Marvellous . . . makes the mythological heroes seem human' – *Today*

Also by Marion Zimmer Bradley in Sphere Books – don't miss:

THE MISTS OF AVALON
THE CATCH TRAP
NIGHT'S DAUGHTER
LYTHANDE

0 7474 0126 8   GENERAL FICTION   £3.99

DEREK TANGYE

JEANNIE
A LOVE STORY

When Jeannie and Derek Tangye withdrew to a cliff-top flower farm in Cornwall, sophisticated London society protested, but an even wider circle was enriched by the enchanted life which they shared and which Derek recorded in the *Minack Chronicles*. Jeannie died in 1986, and, in tribute to her extraordinary personality, her husband has written this portrait of their marriage. The delight of the *Minack Chronicles* is here – the daffodils, the donkeys and the Cornish magic. And all the fizzle and pop of champagne days at the Savoy is captured as Jeannie dazzles admirers from Danny Kaye to Christian Dior.

'All her life she belonged to the glitter, the drama, the heroism and the sacrifice of her time. Jean and Derek have taught a lot of people how to live'
John Le Carré

Don't miss the *Minack Chronicles* by Derek Tangye, also available in Sphere Books

0 7474 0357 0   AUTOBIOGRAPHY   £2.99

THE LODESTONE

Allen Harbinson

**IT IS SAID THAT WHOEVER HOLDS THE
LODESTONE WILL OWN THE ENTIRE WORLD . . .**

It was originally the apex of the Great Pyramid of
Egypt. Its function was to create fusion between Earth
and The Cosmos. It holds the key to the infinite
mysteries of the universe. And it has been missing for
centuries . . .

Wilhelm Zweig, ageing master-criminal, is determined
to find it – and with it the key to immortality . . .

But in his way stands the legendary Count de Saint
Germain, history's most mysterious figure, believed to
be the protector of the magical stone. And against him
is Jerry Remick, a young American with a passion for
unexplained phenomena – and for Zweig's daughter
Ingrid. Relentlessly pursued by Zweig, Jerry and
Ingrid embark upon a dangerous quest for the
Lodestone, a voyage that takes them through Europe
and the Orient to a final magical confrontation on the
summit of the Earth . . .

0 7474 0006 7   FANTASY   £3.99

STEPPING

NANCY THAYER

Stepping isn't easy. It means making friends with two blue-eyed, angel-faced enemies – your husband's children from a former marriage. And taking the steps that bring you close to what you want – home, husband, children, career, friends . . . everything.

For Zelda, loving, irresistible, a woman firmly grounded in the 'eighties, the journey requires a special kind of courage to face the pain and exhilaration of relationships bound by ties that are both more and less than blood.

STEPPING is a powerful and compulsively readable story which explodes the myths of stepmotherhood and crystallises the experiences of the modern woman in today's world.

'Moving, inspiring, a delight'
Publishers Weekly

0 7221 8419 0   GENERAL FICTION   £2.95

MORNING
Nancy Thayer

'There he was, the perfect husband, and here she sat in the tub, not pregnant, the imperfect wife. The flawed wife. The inferior wife. The rapidly-mentally-deteriorating wife. She wanted to break all the dishes over his perfect, understanding, optimistic, loving, helpful head'.

But it wasn't Steve's fault. It was nobody's fault that she couldn't have the child she so desperately wanted. So Sara channelled her energies into her work as an editor. And then she read a manuscript that led her to a creative life of a different kind; the autobiographical novel of a beautiful, terrifying recluse with a mysterious past . . . and a painful obsession.

Also by Nancy Thayer in Sphere Books:

NELL
STEPPING
THREE WOMEN
BODIES AND SOULS

0 7474 0104   GENERAL FICTION   £3.50

BARBARA ERSKINE

Kingdom of Shadows

Clare Royland: rich, beautiful and unhappy, the childless wife of a City banker, obsessed by her ancestress and a strange, inexplicable dream . . .

1306: Isobel, Countess of Buchan, persecuted for her part in crowning Robert the Bruce, her lover . . .

Duncairn Castle: Isobel's home, Clare's heritage, a battle ground for passions spanning the centuries . . .

'Compulsively readable – storytelling at its best'
Today

0 7474 0130 6   GENERAL FICTION   £4.99